TRISTA'S TRUTH

SAVAGE HELL MC BOOK 7

K.L. RAMSEY

JOEL

JOEL WALKED INTO SAVAGE HELL TO FIND AXEL AND MELODY sitting up at the bar, the last thing he wanted was a night out, but he had promised his former partner and her new husband that he'd meet them for a beer to celebrate them getting hitched. Actually, they had been married for almost six months now, and he had been promising to meet them at Savage Hell, for weeks on end, but he was always too tired after his shift to join them for a few beers. He planned to cancel on them again tonight but then, he ran into Melody, and she threatened to hunt him down and drag his ass into the bar for a night out. He protested, saying that he was tired and just wanted to collapse into bed, but she reminded him that tomorrow was Saturday and he'd be able to sleep in. She took away any argument that he had and not showing up wasn't an option.

As soon as Axel and Melody saw him, they smiled and waved in unison, and he could feel his eyes roll. He found what everyone else thought of as adorable, to be annoying, although he kept that to himself. He'd never want them to think that he was jealous about the two of them being together. Melody was not just his partner on the force, she was also his ex-girlfriend. She was the one who had gotten away, and he might be over losing her, but he still didn't find her and her new husband to be cute, adorable, or a perfect couple as others had called them.

"Good to see that you could make it," Melody said.

"Well, I didn't like the alternatives presented to me earlier today, if I didn't show up," he grumbled.

"Tell me you didn't threaten the guy, honey," Axel said.

"She came into my office today to let me know that turning down your invitation again would end up with a manhunt—involving yours truly and your new, blushing bride."

Axel chuckled, seeming to miss the point of Melody telling her new boss that she'd hunt him down and drag his ass to the bar, to be completely inappropriate. "I think your idea of funny and my idea of funny are very different," Joel grumbled. He waved down the bartender, asked for another round of beers, and sat up on the barstool next to Axel.

"Well, getting you here tonight was kind of important to us," she said.

"Why's that?" Joel asked.

"We have someone that we want you to meet," Melody said.

"No," Joel simply said. "No setups. I thought that we've been through all of this before. I don't want to date right now. I just don't have time for it since my promotion. You know how many hours I put in at the station. I don't have time for any extracurriculars," Joel insisted.

"I know how hard you work, Joel," Melody said. "It's why I want to introduce you to my friend, Trista. She's perfect for you and you can't be serious about not dating. Work can't be your entire life. You need to find a work/personal life balance, or you'll wake up one day, all alone, and it will be too late."

"I have some time before that happens, Melody," he assured.

"You're turning forty this year, Joel. You need to diversify, branch out and maybe, just maybe you'll realize that work isn't everything," Melody insisted.

"Just give Trista a chance," Axel chimed in. He knew that he wasn't going to get the final word in all of this. Once Melody set her mind to something, she'd find a way to make it happen. And with Axel taking her side, she'd be relentless.

"Fine," Joel mumbled. "I'll meet this friend of yours, but I'm making no promises," he said.

"At least have a beer with her," Axel said. "Talk to her, maybe even get to know the woman a little bit. She might surprise you, man." He hated surprises, and he had half a mind to tell Axel that, but it was too late. They had roped him into the bar only to ambush him with a fix-up. This whole evening was turning into one giant surprise, and he hated everything about it.

"I know that this is way out of your comfort zone, Joel," Melody said. "But I worry about you. We were close once, and just because that didn't work out doesn't mean that I don't still worry about you."

"While I appreciate that, Melody," he said. "I hate surprises—you know that. Remember how I reacted to that surprise birthday party you threw me at the precinct?"

"Oh, I remember that birthday," Melody said. "You shouted at me for about ten minutes and then stormed out of the break room. You were a jerk, but we ate your cake anyway, and eventually, you got over it."

"I've never gotten over it if we're being honest here. I hate surprises, and now, you're having me meet a complete stranger at a bar and you think it's a good thing?" he asked.

"Just don't throw a fit and stomp out of here," Melody said.

"No promises," he said.

Melody popped up from her barstool and squealed, clapping her hands. "She's here," she gushed.

"As if we couldn't tell," Axel teased. She ran across the bar and hugged her friend. "Trista's not bad looking, right?"

He turned around to look her over, knowing full well that he was going to find her wanting no matter what she looked like. He was being an ass and that had everything to do with how tired he was. "She's not bad," Joel admitted. She was more than not bad but admitting that out loud would be equivalent to admitting that Melody might be right and that was a dangerous game to play. She loved to make him tell her that she was right, at any cost, and he usually tried like hell to avoid having to do it.

Melody and Trista walked across the barroom and just about every guy in the place watched them make their way over to the bar. Trista was a beautiful woman, but that didn't make any of this setup feel right to him.

"Joel," Melody said, her arm around her friend, "this is Trista Stonewell. Trista, this is Joel Swensen."

"It's good to meet you," Trista said, holding out her hand to him. He took her hand into his own, noting the way his skin felt a bit tingly just by her touch.

"Good to meet you too, Trista," Joel said. He sat there like an idiot, holding onto her hand, not realizing that he hadn't let go of it until she pulled it free from his.

"Can I buy you a beer?" he asked.

Trista shook her head and reached into her purse, pulling out a gun and pointing it at his chest. "No, thank you," she said.

"What the hell?" Melody shouted. "What are you doing?"

"What I have to do," Trista whispered. "I'm sorry Melody."

TRISTA

TRISTA WASN'T SURE HOW THIS WAS SUPPOSED TO GO. HER instructions were clear—find Joel Swensen and bring him in alive, by any means necessary. Keeping her job a secret from her friend while she got close to Joel's ex-partner wasn't easy. Working for the CIA was something that she loved but lying for a living wasn't something that she enjoyed doing. She looked at it as part of the job—lying to her friends and family had become a part of her life, even if she hated doing it.

"You will need to come with me Mr. Swensen," Trista ordered.

"And why would I do that?" Joel asked. His slight smirk told her that he thought he had the upper hand in all of this, but he was wrong. He might be a good cop, but she was better. It's why she eventually was recruited to join the CIA.

"For your own safety," she insisted.

Joel barked out his laugh, "It seems to me that the only person threatening my safety is you, honey," he said.

"How about you put the gun down and tell us what this is all about, Trista?" Axel asked.

"Can't," Trista said. If she involved Axel and Melody in this, they wouldn't be safe. She needed to get Joel out of there and then, hope that nobody was following her. It was going to be her best option to keep him safe. The men that he had looking for him were bad news and if she involved her friends, they'd be next on their list of targets.

"It wouldn't be safe for either of you to get involved in this," she breathed. She pulled her badge out of her jacket pocket and quickly flashed it at them. "I'm CIA and you're in trouble, Joel."

"So, it's Joel now?" he asked. "What happened to Mr. Swensen?"

"If I'm going to help you, we should be on a first-name basis. The men who are after you won't care what I call you, really," she said.

"Men who are after me?" he questioned. "And who might they be?"

"The Gemini Brothers," she leaned in to whisper. "I believe that you took down their gang's leader a few months ago, and they're looking for retribution."

"Why would any of this be on the CIA's radar?" Joel asked.

"Because we had a man on the inside when you took

down the lead suspect. We need your help releasing Dante Gemini so that we can bring down their entire operation. It's the only way to stop them and their human trafficking ring."

"Wait, you said that the Gemini Brothers were after me, but this is about letting a known murderer go?" he asked. "Why would I do that?"

"Because the Gemini Brothers are after the same thing. They want Dante released from prison, but they won't stop there. They'll kill anyone close to you to get you to comply, and when you do, they'll murder you too. If you agree to work with me and the CIA, we'll get him released, but no one will have to end up dead."

"Except the countless people who get in Dante's way. What happens when he's free and goes on a revenge-killing spree?" Joel asked. "Because you and I both know that's what will happen, Trista."

She shrugged, "We just have to be one step ahead of him and keep anyone else from getting killed. The CIA needs time to be able to bring him and his family down. We want all of the big players, not just the head of the family. Dante being in prison doesn't make him less powerful. They just put another head in place and Dante controls the family from prison. You have to be smart enough to understand that, Joel. I mean, you seem like a bright guy."

"Gee, thanks for that," Joel grumbled.

"You know what I mean, Joel. I didn't intend to insult you in any way. I need you to come with me—you're not safe here. And everyone around you is in danger. Do you want that for Melody and Axel?" Trista asked.

"Oh—so now you care about me and my husband?" Melody questioned. "You used me to get to Joel. I thought that you were my friend, Trista," she spat.

"I was your friend," she breathed. "I'd still like to be, but the unfortunate part of my job is that sometimes, I have to lie to my friends."

"By lie, you mean you have to make up an entirely different life to feed to me, right? You told me that you're a nurse," she said. "That's what you do for a living, right? You lie."

"Well, it wasn't totally a lie. I was a nurse at one point—in the military. I served my time, and when I got out, I decided that I didn't want to become a private practice nurse, so I went into the police academy instead. I was good at being a cop, and that's when the CIA took notice of me and hired me to be an agent. There, now you know everything that there is to know about me," Trista promised.

Melody stuck her nose up in the air and made a little humming noise. "I'm sure that isn't the case. I'm betting that you have a few more secrets that you aren't sharing with us." She had a lot more secrets, too many to tell, and that's the way she'd keep it too.

She looked back over at Joel as if effectively dismissing Melody and her comments. "So, what's it going to be, Joel?" she asked. She was still holding her gun at him, pointing it at his chest, but she thought that she'd at least let him believe that he had a choice in the matter. The truth of it was that she wasn't going to leave the bar without Joel by her side. Those were her orders and she always followed orders to the letter.

"You going to stay here and possibly get all of these people killed or are you going to come with me and help out the CIA?" she asked.

"Do I really have a choice in the matter?" he grumbled. She wanted to tell him that he didn't, but that would just be like rubbing salt in his wounds. Joel didn't seem like the type of man who took orders from others well. In fact, she was sure of it with the way that he had worked his way up the ranks to Captain so quickly.

"If I told you yes, you wouldn't believe me," she said.

"Probably because it would be another lie," Joel hissed. "Fine, let's get this shit show over with. I'll tell your superiors what I've already told you. I can't just release Dante Gemini. I'm not the person to give that order. You think that I have more power than I actually do, Trista."

She laughed, "You and I both know that's just not true, Joel. You have all the power here," she assured.

"Yet, you're the one pointing a gun at me," he accused. He stood and nodded to Melody and Axel. "Thanks for a great night out, guys," he drawled. "And thanks so much for introducing me to Trista, it's been a blast." She nodded for him to walk in front of her so that she could keep her gun pointed at his back.

"Let's go, Joel," she said. "We have a long drive ahead of

us." She didn't bother to look back at either Melody or Axel. She knew that she had burned her bridges with her new friends and there would be no point. All she needed to focus on now was getting Joel back to headquarters in one peace and knowing the Gemini Brothers, that was going to take a freaking miracle.

JOEL

"You're going to drive," Trista insisted. "You want to take your vehicle or mine?" she asked.

"Mine," he breathed. At least in his own vehicle, he'd have a fighting chance.

"Stop," she said, "where are your keys?" she asked.

"Right pocket," he said. She reached into his pocket and dug around for his keys. "Sure, take your time, sweetheart," he teased. "Just a little bit to the left and I think that you'll find it."

"You're an ass, you know that right?" she asked.

"So I've been told," he said. "I'd really like to tell you that I'm not enjoying this, but I am." She smiled and pulled his keys out of his pocket, holding them up to jingle triumphantly in front of his face.

"Got them," she boasted.

"And here things were just starting to get good," he teased. He knew that knocking her off of her game might be his way to get her to let her defenses down. Unfortunately for him, Trista didn't seem to get frazzled very easily.

She handed him the keys and told him to get in, and he did. She kept her gun trained on him as she rounded the front of his car and got into the passenger side. She buckled and nodded at him to do the same. "Safety first," he mumbled to himself. "You do know how ironic it is that you want me to put on my seatbelt while you're holding a gun to my side, right?" he asked.

"Whatever, just drive, Joel," she spat. He turned on the car and chuckled to himself as he buckled his seatbelt and put the car in drive.

"Where to?" he asked.

"Your precinct," she said. "You're going to release Dante Gemini, as we discussed, and then, I have orders to get you to a safe house, because the Gemini Brothers are going to be coming for you, Joel, whether you like it or not."

"Um, not," Joel said. "And we never discussed me releasing Dante Gemini. You pulled a gun on me and insisted —no discussion."

"Well, I didn't think that you'd be very reasonable, and here I was right," she said. "If I would have walked into that bar and asked you nicely, would you have agreed to my request?" she asked.

"Not in a million fucking years," he growled. "You have no idea what I had to do to put Dante Gemini away." He wasted three years of his life tracking down that asshole and to turn around and have to let him out now felt like a giant slap in the face. "Does the CIA actually believe that letting Gemini out is actually a good idea? They are aware of who he is, right?"

"We're aware," she assured. "We know how much this must pain you, but we need him out so that he can resume his human trafficking business and our guy on the inside will be able to bring down the whole operation. That's the way that it should have been from the start, but then your little local precinct got involved and fucked that all up."

"I'm not following," he said, "if the CIA was involved in the investigation against the Gemini Brothers from the start, why wasn't I told to back down? My precinct would have done so, out of respect for your agency."

"I'm sure that they would," Trista drawled. "You guys are always so very helpful whenever we call you to help out on a case. You do know that my office did call and tell your precinct to back down, right? I mean, we had a guy on the inside and you charging in to arrest Dante Gemini fucked up years of undercover work."

"Your office called to tell us to stand down?" he asked.

"Yep, and two days later, you arrested Dante yourself. So, tell me again how we should have just called you guys," she sassed.

"I had no idea, Trista," he said. "I would have never overstepped if I had gotten that message, but I didn't. I had no idea that you had a man on the inside."

"His name was Peter Stonewell, and he was a good man," she said.

"Was he your husband or your brother?" Joel asked. For some crazy reason, he was hoping that she'd say that he was her brother.

"Brother," she whispered. "Pete was my younger brother and when the Gemini Brothers found out that they had a mole on the inside, they tore their organization apart until they found Pete. They murdered him and sent my brother back to the CIA piece by piece."

"And now, you want your revenge," Joel breathed. He would want the same if the Gemini Brothers did that to one of his family members. Revenge was something that he could understand.

"Partially," she admitted. "I'm still following orders from my superiors if that's what you're wondering, but lucky for me, the CIA and I both want the same thing—Dante Gemini released so that he can lead us right back to his human trafficking ring."

"What makes you think that he'll cooperate with the CIA once you release him?" Joel asked.

Trista shrugged, "I don't," she admitted. "I'm not going to even approach him. He needs to believe that he got out on a technicality. One of our guys is going to pose as a lawyer for the precinct, and he'll explain everything to Dante. He'll tell him that he's free to go because the arresting officer, that's you, didn't follow protocol, and all charges are being dropped."

"I followed the fucking protocol," Joel shouted.

"Noted, and for the record, I believe you, Joel," Trista said. "But Dante doesn't know that you followed protocol. He'll believe that his lawyers worked their magic and did what he's paying them to do. Dante will believe that he got lucky this time, and he'll count it as a win. Those guys always think that they are luckier than they actually are. It's why they try to pull so much shit and get away with it. Let's let him believe what he needs to, and then, when he goes back into the Gemini Brothers, to claim his rightful place as the head of the family, he'll lead us right to his trafficking ring. He's the head of trafficking for the Gemini family and when he resumes business, we'll be there to take down the whole organization this time, not just one man."

"I thought that by bringing in Dante, the Gemini Brothers would fold," Joel admitted. He believed that by bringing down the head of the family, the rest would just crumble, but he was wrong apparently.

"You might have cut off the head of the serpent, but two more grew in its place. It's the way that things work with the Gemini Brothers. They always have a backup plan, and they are always out for blood. This time, it's your blood that they want, Joel. If you think that I'm out for revenge, wait until the Gemini Brothers catch up with you."

"Shit," he mumbled under his breath. If Trista was right, he was in more danger than he'd thought, and working with her and the CIA might be his only way out. "You can put the gun down," he insisted, "I'll work with you, Trista."

"Great," she said, not bothering to put her gun away. "But if we're going to work together, there's something that you should know about me, Joel—I don't trust anyone. The gun stays until you release Dante. Then, if you still want my help, I'll get you someplace safe, as I promised."

"Suit yourself," he said. Joel pulled into his spot in front of the precinct and cut the engine. "But there's something you should know, too, Trista. You won't be able to walk into that building with a gun. You'll set off every alarm in the place and they'll throw your ass in a cell so fast, it will make your head spin. How about you give me a little bit of trust here, and I promise, we'll avenge your brother together? I'm partially responsible for his death. If I had been given that message to stand down, things might have ended differently for your brother. I'm sorry for the part that I played in his death."

Her lip quivered, the only sign that he was getting through to her. She had no reason to trust him, but he wasn't about to screw her over. They wanted the same thing now that he knew the truth, she'd just have to decide if she trusted him or not. "Thank you for saying that, but I don't blame you, Joel. I blame the Gemini Brothers and when I find out which one of those fuckers killed my brother, I'm going to put a bullet between their eyes." He believed that she would too. Trista didn't seem like the kind of woman to make empty threats.

"Got it," he said. "Are you coming in with me, or do you want to wait here?" he asked.

Trista shook her head at him and sighed, holstering her gun. "I'm coming in," she grumbled. "Don't fuck this up for me, Joel. I won't hesitate to pull my gun in there. You can stick me in a cell, but I won't be in there for very long," she insisted. "My guys at the CIA will have me out of there so fast, your head will spin," she said, giving him back his words.

Joel chuckled and nodded, "Duly noted, Ma'am," he drawled. "Let's go," he ordered. He didn't bother to look back to see if Trista was following him. He could hear her sexy heels clicking on the pavement behind him.

They took the elevator up from the lobby to the fifth floor and he noticed that Trista seemed a bit nervous. She looked young to be a CIA agent, but he knew from what she told Melody about her time in the military that she was probably in her late twenties. Compared to him, she was practically a kid. Joel never thought of himself as old until he got shot on the job a few years back. He was turning forty later that year, and to him, that sounded ancient.

"How old was your brother?" he asked, making small talk.

"He was only twenty-seven," she said. "He had only been with the CIA for a little over a year, and God, he loved his job."

"I'm sorry," Joel breathed, "that's so young."

"It was," she said. "I just turned thirty-one and I never thought that I'd see thirty. When I was serving in the military, I thought for sure that I'd be the one being sent home to my parents in a body bag, not Pete."

"Was it just the two of you?" Joel asked.

"Yeah," Trista breathed, "how about you? Any brothers or sisters?"

"I have three younger brothers and a sister," Joel said. "My poor mother wanted a girl, so she convinced my father to keep trying. She got four boys to drive her crazy, but she finally had her girl. Not that my little sister is any better behaved than my brothers."

"So, you're the oldest then?" she asked.

"Yep," he said, "I'm turning forty this year and they're dying to throw me an over-the-hill party—you know the one, right? They'll have tombstones with my name on them and black balloons everywhere." Joel smiled at the thought of it. His siblings were talking about the party that they wanted to throw him when they all saw each other at his youngest brother's twenty-eight birthday party a few weeks back. He pretended to be put off by the whole idea, but he had to admit, it sounded kind of fun. Even his mom and dad got in on the razing and came up with a few ideas for the party.

"Sounds fun," she said. The elevator doors opened, and he stepped off. The office seemed pretty quiet tonight. He nodded to his desk and told her to follow him, and Trista did. Hopefully, they'd get in and out without much fanfare.

"I'll just need to put the order in on my laptop," he said. "It's a bit of paperwork, but it shouldn't take too long. You want coffee or anything?" he asked.

"I'm good," Trista said, looking around the place. "I just want to get this over with." He felt the same way, but she seemed a bit more nervous than he felt. "Do you know all of these people?" she asked.

Joel quickly looked around the place and back to her, nodding. "Pretty much. I mean, I don't recognize some of the people in custody right now, but the officers, I know well. Why?" he asked.

"Just making sure that we're safe is all," she said. Joel sat down behind his desk and Trista stood in the corner, against the wall as if to keep an eye on everyone around them.

"You know, you can have a seat," he offered.

"I'm good," she said.

"Right, because you're not garnering any extra attention by standing back in the corner like that, honey," he mumbled under his breath.

"I heard that," Trista whispered. "And I'm not your honey."

"Noted," he said. Joel found the forms that he needed to send over to the prison to get Dante Gemini released. "Once I hit send, this will happen pretty quickly. Is your guy in place?" he asked. Having one of her men pose as a precinct lawyer to meet Dante and tell him that they had made a mistake was brilliant. A guy as smart as Dante would want an explanation and telling him that they had fucked up was a good one. He'd believe that because there was no way that Dante would ever accept his own faults or failures.

"He's there now, waiting for my order to go in. You just give the word, and I'll send him in," Trista said. "We'll be able to hear and see everything on my phone. My guy is wired, and I have access to the video footage at the prison." She pulled her phone out and send her guy a message to be ready and sat on the edge of his desk. "Ready for the show?" she asked.

"As I'll ever be," he assured. Honestly, he wasn't ready for any of this, but ready or not, this mess was coming for him, and he needed to get ready if he planned on staying alive.

TRISTA

"My guy says that he's in the holding cell, waiting for them to bring in Dante," Trista said, reading his text message out loud.

"Are you sure that this will work?" Joel asked.

"Not a clue, but it's all we have to go on. We need for Dante to believe that it's safe for him to resume business as usual, or we're all fucked. We will have let out a man who's guilty as hell, for nothing. We can't let that happen."

"We won't let that happen," Joel assured. "I promise. I fucked this up and now, I plan on helping to fix it."

"Shh," she said, nodding to her phone, "they just brought Dante into the room. I want to listen." Joel stood next to her, and she held her phone between the two of them, so he could watch with her.

"Who the hell are you?" Dante asked her agent, Ed Adams, who was posing as a lawyer.

"I'm one of the lawyers here on staff for the correctional facility," Ed said.

"What do you want?" Dante asked. "I'm not going to talk to you without my lawyer here, so you're wasting your time if that's what you're after."

"It's not," Ed said, "I'm here to let you know that you are being released." Dante looked Ed over as if he didn't believe a word that he was saying, and Trista couldn't blame the guy. She'd be skeptical too if she was being released for no reason.

"Why would you all just let me go?" Dante asked. "When I was arrested, I was told that the plan was to toss me in a cell and throw away the key. What's changed?" Dante asked.

"While we were building our case against you, our team realized that there were mistakes made in your arrest that won't stand up in court. It's enough to get your case dismissed, and we have no choice but to let you go."

"Mistakes," Dante repeated, "I should have known. So, I'm getting out of here because the guy who arrested me fucked up?"

"You could say that," Ed agreed, "although we'd never admit to that in court. It's why we're willing to just release you now and save all of us the time and energy of a court case."

"I see," Dante said, "so, I'm just free to leave? I mean, I don't have to check in with anyone, or any of that shit?"

"Nothing else will be required of you," Ed said, "we'll get the paperwork ready, and you'll be free to go within the hour. For now, you'll be taken back to your cell to await discharge."

"All right then," Dante said. The guy looked happier than a kid who got what he asked for on Christmas morning. He had no clue that he was being set up, and that's just the way that they needed to keep it.

"Will you pass on a message to the officer who arrested me?" Dante asked.

"Um sure," Ed promised. Trista looked Joel over, worried about what Dante was about to say.

"Great—tell him that I appreciate the assist." Hearing Dante say that Joel helped him out in any way, made her sick, but she needed to remember that this was all just part of the game. They needed to pretend that Joel fucked up so that Dante could get out of prison and go on with business as usual. Still, it had to be a hard pill to swallow.

Trista turned off her phone and put it back into her pocket. "You all right?" she asked.

"No, but I will be," Joel said. "I hate letting that guy think that I fucked up and that's why he's getting out of jail. If I had things my way, he'd rot in a cell for the rest of his damn life."

"I get it," Trista said, "I really do, but we need his whole organization, and that can only happen if Dante's out of prison."

"What happens next?" Joel asked. "I mean, we got Dante out, what next?"

"Next, you and I have to go into hiding while we wait for him to slip up again," Trista said.

"No," Joel said, "there's no way that I'm going to hide away while we wait him out. I have a life to live and a precinct to run. I can't go into hiding with you."

"All right, suit yourself," Trista said. "But don't come crying to me when the Gemini Brothers land on your doorstep. They're not going to stop coming for you just because Dante is out, Joel."

"Well, I'll take my chances," he said. "Besides, I can take care of myself. I've gotten this far, haven't I?" he asked.

"Do what you want," Trista said acting as if she didn't care, but she did. She wasn't lying when she told Melody that she liked her. Even though she had to lie to her new friend, she knew that she was doing the right thing. Trista would never want to do anything to hurt someone whom Melody cared about, and she cared about Joel.

Trista called Melody and when she let the call go to voice-mail for the fifth time, she knew that she should just give up. Trista wasn't usually one to give up so easily, but she needed to get back to her place, pack her bags and head out of town to the safe house that her office secured for her. She was hoping to give Melody a heads up so that she could help keep an eye on Joel, but she couldn't do that if she didn't answer the phone and let Trista explain. She'd just have to stop by his place, to make sure that he knew what he was up against, before heading out of town. If Joel still refused to leave with her, she'd know that she did all she could to help him.

She packed her bag and was on her way out when her cell phone rang. "This better be good, Trista," Melody spat. "The only reason I'm calling you back is that I've been trying to reach Joel all night, and he's not answering his phone. What did you do to him?"

"Nothing," Trista assured, "I left him at the precinct about an hour ago. I was going to swing by his place on my way out of town, to make sure that he's all right."

"Yeah, well, I don't think that he's okay, Trista," Melody spat. "You kidnapped him and now, I can't get in touch with him. What am I supposed to believe?" Melody asked.

"I know that asking you to believe me, is a long shot, but if you could, that would be great. I told Joel that it was a bad idea to go back to his place. Maybe he took my advice and went into hiding. The Gemini Brothers won't give up trying to find him, but he's stubborn and won't listen to reason."

"Well, you've only been on one date, but you seem to have him pegged," Melody teased.

"I'd hardly call what we did tonight, going on a date. He helped me free Dante Gemini, and then, we went our separate ways. He didn't even buy me dinner," Trista said.

"So, I'm assuming that you didn't get our good night kiss then?" Melody asked. She was taunting Trista, trying to knock her off of her game, but she wouldn't allow that.

Trista needed to keep her head clear if she was going to get out of town tonight as planned.

"Listen, I'm headed out of town, and I'd advise you to get Joel to do the same if you want to keep your friend alive," Trista said.

"When I find Joel, I'll tell him your concerns," Melody assured. "I'm sure that he'll take them to heart. Listen, we're not friends, Trista, and we won't be friends. You lied to me, and I don't handle liars well. I'd appreciate it if you just didn't contact me again, please."

"Whatever you say, Melody," Trista agreed. She wasn't about to argue with the woman, she was right, Trista had lied to her about who she was. It didn't stop the pain that she felt about being blown off though, and Trista had a feeling that nothing would help her get over it.

It was late, and Trista felt about ready to drop. It felt like weeks since she walked into Savage Hell to meet Joel for their supposed date. It felt like a lifetime had passed since she held him at gunpoint and got him to agree to release Dante Gemini. Now, she was on her way out of town, driving to the safe house, but first, she wanted to stop and check on Joel. Honestly, she wanted to give him one last chance to leave with her, but she had a feeling that she already knew what his answer was going to be. He was as stubborn as they came, and for some odd reason, that turned her completely on. She always liked a man who'd stand his ground and made her work a bit to get him to notice her. It kept her on her toes, and Trista needed that in her life—someone to challenge her.

Not that Joel had signed up for that in any way. As soon as she told him that he was free to go, earlier that evening, he ran out of the precinct like his pants were on fire. Sure, maying holding the guy at gunpoint, instead of asking for his help upfront, wasn't her finest decision, but she felt as though she had no other choice. Maybe she should have led him on, and asked him back to her place, instead of kidnapping him and demanding that he help her. The problem with that plan was that it wasn't Trista's style. She was a push-through kind of woman. If something stood in her way, she found a way through it, not around it. Demanding that Joel go with her to the precinct while holding a gun in his side was more her speed, and unfortunately, it also earned her a lot of enemies.

Trista pulled up to the address she had for Joel. Using the CIA's resources to track people down, was one of her great pleasures in life. She loved being able to find anyone, anywhere. As soon as she got out of her car, Trista knew that something was off. She had pretty good instincts and usually, trusting them got her out of sticky situations.

Trista pulled her gun from her shoulder holster and rounded the side of the house, deciding to go in through the back door. She just hoped that if someone was in the house with Joel, they wouldn't have noticed her pulling up to the place. She pushed her way into the already opened back door and cleared the kitchen. There was no sign of foul play, but there was also no sign of Joel either.

She wanted to call out to him but knew that wasn't a good idea. Alerting anyone that she was there wouldn't work in giving her the element of surprise. She walked through the dark house and wondered if Joel was even home. If he wasn't, why was his back door open? Trista cleared the family and dining room and looked up the stairs to where she knew whoever was in the house would be waiting for her. Trista was about to go up the staircase when a hand grabbed her arm. "Don't," a man's voice whispered into her ear. She turned to find Joel holding her back from going up to the second floor.

"What's going on?" she whispered.

"Someone's in the house," he breathed. "The back door was open when I got home."

"Do you know who it is?" she asked.

"I'm assuming one of Dante's men, but I can't be sure. You stay here and I'll go up," he insisted.

"Not a chance," Trista whispered. "You stay here, and I'll go up. They obviously want you since they are at your house."

"Right, so if you go up there, they'll just kill you to get to me," Joel insisted.

"How many men are there?" she asked.

"No clue," he whispered.

"Fine, we'll go up together and figure it out from there. You go left and I'll go right," he said. Trista was sure that Joel was sending her straight into a closet or bathroom, but she didn't care. At least he was letting her participate. They walked up the stairs, side by side, and when they got to the top, she went left, just as Joel ordered. She cleared a spare bedroom and a bathroom, as well as the hallway closet.

"Trista," Joel called, "you'll want to see this," he said. She quickly walked down the hallway to what she assumed was his master bedroom.

"All clear?" she asked.

"Yeah, but someone was here. They left me their calling card." She looked inside the box that he held open to her and almost gagged when she saw a hand with a note that said, "You had a hand in what happened to Dante. You're next."

"Shit," Trista breathed. "I told you that they were going to come after you, Joel. You need to come with me," she insisted, tugging at his arm.

"Not a chance," he said. "If they want to come for me, they'll know where to find me here. Listen, I got a notification that someone was in my house before I even pulled into my driveway. I say we beef up my already good security system and you and I stay right here. We need to be close in case something happens with Dante, and we need to move our teams in. Plus, I don't want to run. I don't want to constantly be looking back over my shoulder to see what's coming for me. Do you?" he asked.

"Damn it," she grumbled. She didn't want to run either. She was never one to run away from a fight, and now, she was planning on doing just that. Joel was right, she wanted to know who was coming for her and when. "You're right," she agreed.

"I'm sorry," Joel said, cupping his ear to her. "I couldn't quite hear you. What did you say?"

"I said that you're right," she hissed. "I don't like having to say it once, please don't make me repeat myself, Joel." He chuckled as he holstered his gun.

"I say that we get this place secured and then, you and I can work on getting my security up to what it will need to be to take on Dante and his men when he makes good on his promise to come for me next. I think we'll need a bit of help with that part. You mind if I call over a few buddies who can help us?" Joel asked.

"As in your MC friends from that bar Melody had me meet you at?" Trista asked. He didn't seem like the MC type. Hell, Joel seemed as clean-cut as they came, and meeting him at that biker bar tonight kind of threw her off of her game.

"Yeah, if you don't mind them coming over here. Some of the guys specialize in security and the faster we do this, the faster we can get some shut eye."

"All right," Trista agreed.

"Great—you can take that room at the end of the hall. You cleared it when you came up here," he said.

"I know the one," she said, "thanks, Joel." Trista wasn't sure if staying at his place was a good plan, but there was safety in numbers, and she knew that Joel seemed like the type of guy that would have her back, no matter what was coming for them. She needed someone in her corner like him if she was going to bring down the Gemini Brothers and avenge her little brother's death.

JOEL

Joel called Savage and filled him in on what was happening. Savage promised to round up a couple of the guys and be over within the hour to help him upgrade his security. He asked Joel if he was sure that he didn't want to disappear, that he had some guys who could help with that, but Joel assured him that he was good to stay put.

After he got off the phone with Savage, he gave Axel a call to let him know what was happening. He and Melody both insisted on coming over to help out with the security, and he had to admit, he was grateful. Melody was a damn good cop and knowing that she'd have his back helped put his mind at ease a bit.

"Everything set up?" Trista asked as she walked into the kitchen. She had been unpacking up in his spare room and he was kicking himself for not giving her his bed. The spare room's bed was a bit uncomfortable—something that he had always planned on fixing, but he never got around to it. Joel never really needed to since he didn't get many overnight guests.

"Yeah," he said, "Savage is bringing over a few guys. He's the club's Prez and knows what he's doing when it comes to security. I also called Axel and he and Melody are coming over too."

"Great," Trista said, "that way your partner can mean mug me some more and call me a liar."

"Well, she's not wrong," Joel countered, "you did lie to her, right?"

"I did, but I told you that I had no choice. You were in danger, and I needed your help getting Dante freed from prison. If you didn't admit to screwing up during his arrest, he would have never gotten out. By the way, I don't think that I've said this yet, but thanks for taking one for the team. You were great."

He hated having to lie about the arrest. He did things by the book and having a black mark on his record sucked. "Whatever," he mumbled. Trista giggled and he shook his head at her. "Shut up," he grumbled.

"Don't worry, I won't take it personally," she teased. "For the record, telling me to shut up only makes me want to talk more."

"Great," Joel mumbled. "Before everyone gets here, would

you like a sandwich?" He had pulled everything that he had in his refrigerator for sandwiches out and put them on the counter. "I was going to make myself one."

"Sure, if it's not too much of a problem," she said.

"Not at all, and while I make our sandwiches, we can figure out a way for you and Melody to get along," Joel said.

"I don't know if that's going to happen," Trista said, scrunching up her nose. Yeah, he found that totally sexy, but he'd keep that to himself.

"Well, she's a nice person, and once she gets to know you, she'll see that you seem to be nice too," he offered.

"You don't even know me, Joel," Trista reminded. "You think I'm nice?"

"Yeah, I do," he admitted.

"Aww, thanks," she gushed, "I think that you're nice too. Can I ask you a personal question?" He could tell that saying no wouldn't get him far with Trista. She seemed like the type to keep digging around until she got the answers that she was looking for. It would probably be easier to just answer her question instead of giving her any fight.

"Um, sure," he hesitantly answered.

"I know why I let Melody fix us up, I needed you to help me get Dante released, but why would you agree to a fix-up? I mean, you seem like a good guy—you're nice, you seem fair, and you're good looking." He flashed her his smile and she shook her head at him. "Jesus, don't make this into a big thing, Joel."

"Right, but you just called me good looking, so there's that," he said.

"Okay, can you just answer the question?" she asked.

"Sure," he said, "I had no idea that Melody was setting me up. I thought that I was just meeting her and her new husband, Axel for a few beers. I had been promising them that we'd get together since their wedding, and well, I was out of excuses and Melody refused to let me cancel on them again."

"So, she set you up with me and you had no idea?" she asked.

"No clue," he agreed, "she sprang the set-up on me when you walked in."

"Well, that's shitty," Trista said.

"No kidding," Joel said, "and then, you walked in and pulled a gun on me. I guess that will teach her to set me up with anyone in the future."

Trista laughed, "I guess so," she agreed.

"Now, can I ask you something?" Joel asked.

"Sure, I'm an open book," she said.

"Are you really looking for a set-up or was tonight purely about getting Dante out of jail? I mean, how did the topic of conversation come up between you and Melody about the two of us meeting?"

"I knew that you were single," Trista admitted. "I did my research on you and when I figured out that you had a very small inner circle of friends, and that you and Melody weren't just partners, but had been together in the past, I hatched the plan to get close to her. I told her that I just couldn't seem to meet any nice guys, and I gushed about how lucky she was to meet Axel. I showed up at Savage Hell a few times, hanging out with the two of them. It's a wonder that you and I never bumped into each other while I was there."

"I didn't get out much. Hell, tonight was one of the first nights in months that I agreed to go out, and I even pitched a fit, trying to get out of it. But Melody put her foot down, and now, I know why. She had set up for the two of us to meet, and if didn't show up, her plan wouldn't work."

"I guess that I should thank Melody for her assistance, then. If she hadn't convinced you to come out tonight, I might have never gotten my chance to free Dante." Trista took the plate that he handed her.

"I hope that turkey is all right," he said, "it's all I had left."

"Turkey is great, thank you," she said, taking a big bite of her sandwich.

"Would you like some water?" he asked. "It's either that or beer and since it's after one in the morning, I think that beer is a bad option."

"Geeze, it's after one?" she asked around a mouthful of sandwich.

"Yep," he said, "I'm hoping that with all of the help we've got coming, it will only take a couple of hours to outfit this place with the new security gear that Savage is bringing over. I'm beat."

"Same," she agreed. "I was looking forward to getting to the safe house and catching some shut eye. Things around the office have been crazy lately, and sleep has been hard to come by."

"Yeah, we've been pretty busy too, lately. I felt about ready to drop when I got back here tonight, but then, I found the back door open, and that sure woke me up," he admitted.

"I'm sure that it did," she said.

"Why did you stop by here tonight?" he asked. "I mean, if you were tired and just wanted to get to the safe house, why stop here?"

"Because I wanted to try, one last time, to get you to come with me. I knew that Dante wasn't going to leave you alone. He was going to come for you whether he thought that you screwed up and gave him a get-out-of-jail-free card, or not. When I got here, I just had a feeling that something wasn't right."

"I get those sometimes too," Joel admitted. "My intuition saved my ass more than a few times over the years."

"Yeah, me too," she said, "and, when I walked around to the back door and found that it was open, I knew that the alarms going off in my head were warranted."

"Yeah, I'm just trying to figure out how they got back out of here without crossing paths with us," Joel said.

"I'm betting that they went out the front door when we were coming in," she said. "I noticed that it wasn't locked on my way up the stairs."

"Yeah, I just thought that they came in that way, but your

theory makes sense," he said. He pulled his cell phone from his pocket and rounded the kitchen island. "I picked up two shadows on my cameras. The pictures are poor quality, but I could make out two of them."

Trista looked at the video feed and nodded. "I count two guys also. You can tell by their build that they are probably men."

"I thought so too," he said. Joel was surprised at how easy it was to work with Trista. He almost expected a fight with her at every turn, but she didn't give him one.

"I'm glad that you agreed to stay here with me," he admitted. "It's nice to know that you'll have my back."

Trista shrugged, "I just thought that there's safety in numbers. If you plan on staying here, you'll need backup," she said.

"Well, thanks for being my backup," he breathed.

"I'll do the dishes while you put the food away," she offered. "The guys should be here soon, and I still have to come up with a way to get Melody to forgive me."

"Don't be upset if that doesn't happen tonight," he said. "Melody can be a tough nut to crack. Just give her some time."

Trista nodded and took his plate from him. "Thanks for the advice, Joel," she said.

Savage had shown up with his husband, Bowie, and Throne tagged along too. Thorne was a new guy at the club, but from what Joel knew about him, he liked him. He was a genius at security and Savage was smart to bring the new guy along.

Axel and Melody showed up shortly after the guys had and Melody gave Trista the stink eye, just as she thought she would. He cornered Melody when Trista was checking in on the guys, and even though he knew better, he asked his partner about forgiving Trista.

"Why should I?" Melody asked. "She lied to me, and in case you've forgotten, she held you at gunpoint just a few hours ago. What—you two are besties now and I'm supposed to just forgive her?"

"No," Trista said from the doorway to the kitchen. "You aren't supposed to just forgive me. I haven't even asked for your forgiveness and Joel asking you for it, doesn't count. I'm truly sorry and would love for you to be able to forgive me someday, but I know that it's going to take some time. For now, all you need to know is that I only did what I had to do to keep Joel safe. He was my assignment. I was supposed to bring him in and get him to release Dante Gemini. Once that was over, my assignment ended. I'm here now as someone who wants to help you both. I want to keep Joel out of the Gemini Brother's hands and to do that, I'm going to have to stay here. But you have my word, I'll keep him safe," Trista said.

Melody barked out her laugh, "You're going to keep Joel

safe?" she asked. Trista nodded and Melody laughed again. "You do know that he's quite capable of taking care of himself, right?" she asked.

"I assume so," Trista said. "But I'm just letting you know; I won't let anyone get to him. I've got his back."

"Isn't that sweet? Joel, I thought that your partner was the one who had your back. Now, you're letting the CIA handle that job?" Melody asked.

"That's not how she meant it, Melody," Joel defended. The last thing he needed was a showdown in his kitchen just before dawn. "Listen, it's late and we're all tired. How about we just table this conversation for another time?" he asked.

Axel joined them and wrapped his arm around his wife. "I agree with Joel. We're all tired and maybe things will look better once we all get some sleep. The guys are finished, and Savage is ready to head out unless you need anything else," Axel said.

"You all have already done so much. I think that we'll be good from here on out," Joel said.

"Are you coming into the office in the morning?" Melody asked.

"Yes," Joel said.

"No," Trista corrected. "You can't go to work. It won't be safe for you or any of your coworkers if you go to work. You need to stay put until I get further intel about where Dante is. Once he got out, he went underground."

"I can't just sit here and wait for him to show his face again, Trista," Joel insisted. "I'm going to work." Trista crossed her arms over her chest, and he couldn't help his smile. "Does that pose usually work for you?" he asked.

"Yes," she sassed.

"Well, it doesn't on me," Joel said.

"I hate to say this, but I agree with Trista," Melody said. "If you put everyone in danger just by coming in, what good will that do?"

"No good at all," Joel grumbled. He felt as though he was being ganged up on, and he hated feeling that way. "Fine, I'll stay put until Trista finds out where Dante is. Does that work for you both?" he asked, looking between Trista and Melody. They both nodded and Axel laughed. "Shut up, asshole," Joel said.

"Hey man," Savage said, sticking his head in the back door, "we're going to head out. You good?" he asked.

"Yeah, we're good," Joel said. "Thanks for everything, man."

"Not a problem," Savage said. "If anything else comes up, don't hesitate to give me a call."

"Will do," Joel agreed.

"We're going to head out too," Axel said, "Melody has to be up in a few hours for work. She won't play hooky, even with the boss being out."

"Good to know," Joel said. "Thank you both for coming out tonight—or this morning. I appreciate it."

"We both do, thank you," Trista agreed.

Melody looked Trista over and he could tell that she was going to say something but thought better of it. "I'll be in touch tomorrow, Joel," she said. "I want to be kept in the loop."

"Of course," Joel agreed. He pulled Melody in for a quick hug and shook Axel's hand. "Thanks for everything guys," he said. He showed them out and turned back to find Trista standing in the corner of the kitchen crying. She was trying to pretend that she wasn't, but he could tell. Joel never knew what to do when any woman cried around him—and Trista was no exception.

"Hey," Joel said.

"I'm all right," she lied. "I'm overly tired and I feel awful about what I had to do to Melody. Lying might be a part of my job, but I hate it." He hated that part of his job too, so he knew exactly how she felt.

"I get it," he said. "How about we get some shut-eye, and things will look better once the sun comes up promise," he said. "Um, about the spare bed," he said. "I forgot to tell you this, but that mattress is awful. If you can't sleep on it, just let me know, and I'll take the sofa."

"And here I was starting to think that you were inviting me into your bed for the night. But then, you went and offered to sleep on the couch, like a gentleman. That's going to take some getting used to. I hang out with guys who are douchebags for the most part."

"Well, thanks for not thinking that I'm a douchebag he said." Joel realized that he had put his hands on her waist when he found her crying, tiring to get her to stop, and they were still there. "Um, sorry," he said.

"For what?" Trista asked.

"For touching you. I didn't mean to," he said.

"Well, that's a shame," she said, "because I kind of liked it, Joel." She went up on her tiptoes and kissed his cheek on her way past him out of the kitchen. "Good night," she called back over her shoulder, and all Joel could do was stand in his kitchen, like a fool, watching her go.

TRISTA

TRISTA WOKE THE NEXT MORNING TO THE SUNSHINE streaming in through the windows. She had forgotten to close the curtains before crawling into bed; she was so tired. She groaned and rolled over, pulling the covers up over her head, trying to fall back to sleep. After about ten minutes of pretending to be asleep, she groaned and rolled back over, pulling her phone from the nightstand where she had left it to charge before going to bed.

"Nine in the morning," she moaned. That meant that she had only gotten about four hours of sleep for the night. "I've survived on less," she said to herself.

Joel peeked his head into her room and smiled. "Sorry, you left your door open," he said.

"And I left my curtains open too," she whined. "I guess

that I just kind of passed out last night. How did you sleep?" she asked.

"Like a log. Do you usually talk to yourself in the morning?" he asked.

"Well, I do live alone, and there's no one else around in the morning or evening for that matter. So, I guess that my answer is yes—I do talk to myself," she said.

"Would you like some coffee?" he asked. "I was about to go down to the kitchen to make some."

"I'd love some coffee," she agreed, "thank you."

"No problem," Joel said.

"Can I take a quick shower first?" she asked.

"Absolutely," he agreed, "I got up about an hour ago and went for a run. I just got out of the shower and was on my way downstairs when I heard you talking to yourself."

"You went running?" she asked, sitting up in bed.

"I did, why?" he asked.

"I thought that you were going to stay put until I could find Dante," she reminded.

"I agreed not to go to work but this was just a run. I didn't put anyone else in danger," he insisted.

"You put yourself in danger," Trista said. "Staying put means staying in the house."

"Well, you can't expect me not to leave the house, Trista," he said. "We'll run out of food."

"You know the routine, Joel," she said. "We stay here and have things delivered, if necessary, but we don't leave. It's not safe."

"Okay, how about you take a shower and I suck down a few cups of coffee, and then, we can discuss all of the ridiculous rules that you want me to follow," he said.

"They aren't ridiculous," she insisted, "they're necessary." God, he was the most infuriating man on the planet.

"Well, I disagree, and we can stand here all morning and debate this, or we can have some coffee and try to find out where Dante went," Joel offered.

"Coffee now, debate later," Trista agreed.

"Good plan," he said, "don't be too long. I can't promise that there will still be coffee left if you take forever in the shower." Trista quickly got out of bed and grabbed her clothes from her suitcase, making Joel chuckle. "You really do love coffee, don't you?" he teased.

"You have no idea," Trista said.

☙ ᵔ ❧

By the time she showered and got down to the kitchen, over half the pot of coffee was gone. "Wow," she whispered, "you weren't joking around about drinking all of the coffee."

"If you need more, I can make another pot," he said. "I'm not used to having to share coffee in my own home. The precinct is another story, although I don't dare drink the coffee there." He made a face that made Trista giggle.

"That bad?" she asked.

"Yeah." She caught Joel looking her over out of the corner of her eye as she poured her cup of coffee, and when she turned to face him, coffee mug in hand, he pretended to notice something on the floor.

"Were you just checking me out?" she boldly asked.

"Um, yeah," he admitted. "You just look different. Last night, you were wearing a pants suit and now—well, you look different."

"Yeah, you've said that twice now," she said. She looked down her body and back up at him. Joel's eyes followed her own and she couldn't help her smile. Last night, when she met him, she was still wearing her work clothes. She usually stuck to business suits—pants, a blouse, and a jacket. It was her uniform of sorts, but when she was at home, she liked to be comfortable. She had on a pair of form-fitting leggings and a crop top that showed off her belly and most of her tattoos.

"I guess I didn't peg you for having tattoos," he said. She kept them hidden at work, not wanting her coworkers to know who she really was. For all they knew, she was confident, capable, and badass. The woman who stood in Joel's kitchen right now was none of those things when she was off duty. She loved her tattoos but had gotten them when she was much younger and didn't have plans on ever doing anything as auspicious as joining the CIA and becoming one of their top agents.

Trista shrugged, "Well, I don't think that my tats should be on display for my co-workers. They're personal, and not for them."

"Who are they for?" Joel asked.

"They are for me," she said. "I got them when I was younger, although this one is kind of new." She held out her arm for him to see and he ran his fingers over her brother's name and the black rose that she had tattooed into the sleeve on her right arm. "I got this one for Pete after Dante had him murdered."

"It's beautiful," Joel said. "You must still really miss him."

"I do, every day," Trista admitted. "There isn't a day that passes that I don't think about him and what Dante did to him. That's why this is so important to me. I want to make the Gemini Brothers pay for what they did to Pete."

"We will find a way to make that happen," Joel promised. It was nice to have someone on her side. It had felt like a long time since she had that happen. Sure, her team at work seemed to understand her drive to bring Dante Gemini to justice, but they were also getting paid to care about the case. Joel wasn't even on the case anymore, technically, because of jurisdiction issues.

"Thank you for saying that," she said. "I appreciate it."

"I mean it, Trista," he said. Joel was still holding her arm and ran his hand down to her hand, taking hers into his own. "I know that we got off to a rocky start," he said.

Trista barked out her laugh, "Yeah, you could say that. I did hold you at gunpoint."

"Well, there was that," Joel teased, "but, I really do want to help you. I hate that this has happened to your family because of me," he said, looking back at Pete's tattoo tribute on her arm.

"You didn't know," she insisted.

"Right, but I moved in too early and got your brother killed and fucked up your investigation. I wish that I could go back in time and change things, but I can't. All I can do now is promise to help you fix them."

"That's enough, Joel," she assured.

"I hope so," he said. "You know, I kind of wish now that last night was just a set-up. I think that I would have liked you, under different circumstances, Trista," he said. As she lay in her bed last night, she had thought the same thing. If last night was truly just a set-up between the two of them, she wouldn't have minded. Joel was the kind of man she needed in her life—not the countless bad boys she had dated.

"I feel the same way, Joel," she admitted. "I don't just think that I would have liked you. I do like you."

"Oh," Joel whispered, taking a step closer to her. Trista wasn't sure what to do next, really, but Joel seemed to have a plan. "So, you like me?" he asked.

"I do," she admitted, "but, as you said, things are complicated. You really should keep your distance from me, Joel."

"What if I like you too, and I don't want to keep my distance?" he asked.

"Joel," she whispered. He leaned down and sealed his mouth over hers and waited her out to comply. It didn't take her long to let him in, wrapping her arms around his neck. She knew that kissing Joel wasn't the best plan, but she didn't care. Trista lived for her job, and now, it was time to do some living for herself—even if it was just a kiss.

Her phone rang and she quickly ended the kiss, taking a step back from him, putting some much-needed space between the two of them. "I better get that in case it's work," she said.

"Of course," he agreed. "I'll make us something to eat while you take your call."

Trista walked into the family room for a bit of privacy and sat down on the sofa with her coffee and cell phone. "Hello," she answered.

"Hi, Trista," her boss said. Henry Alexander was one of the best bosses that she ever had. She loved his no-nonsense, get right down to business kind of guy. They had that in common.

"What can I do for you, boss?" she asked.

"You can tell me what happened last night and why I'm hearing about it through rumors at work this morning," he said. "Why are you still in town?"

"Well, I'm still in town because I made a promise to my friend, Joel, that I'd have his back," she started.

"Friend?" Henry shouted into the phone, "He was your assignment, Trista. You weren't supposed to go and make friends with him."

"Needless to say, the assignment has changed. Joel cooperated with our plan. I didn't need to hold him at gunpoint, as I was ordered to do. He released Dante Gemini on his own accord. He didn't get the order to stand down and not move in to arrest Gemini. Joel had no idea what was going on behind the scenes with the CIA. He felt awful that he interfered with our investigation, so he went along with our plan to get Dante out. He said that he wants to help us bring down the Gemini Brother's whole organization."

"He's out of his jurisdiction," Henry said. "This is a CIA matter now. Plus, I've heard a rumor that their whole organization has been moved, but we can't be sure."

"That would explain why he's seemed to be able to disappear. As soon as he was released, he went off radar, and I can't track him," Trista said.

"Yeah, we've lost track of him and his team too," Henry admitted.

"Well, someone was here last night. When I got to Joel's place, to check on him, his back door was open. We have grainy video footage of two men entering his house, but that's about all we have. He had some of his friends come over to help upgrade his security. Joel said that he won't run, that if Dante wants him, he knows where to find him, and I have to admit, I don't disagree with his take on this mess. Maybe running isn't the answer."

"That's bullshit," Henry insisted, "you two need to go into a safe house to avoid what happened last night, happing again."

"That's the thing, I don't think that Dante's eager to get his hands on either of us. I think that he's got bigger fish to fry, I just can't figure out who." Trista had a feeling that she couldn't shake about Dante going after something or someone bigger than either of them.

"If you won't go to the safe house, I'm afraid that I'll have to remove you from the case," Henry said. "You're too close to it anyway. I should have taken you off the case after Pete died, but I left you on knowing that you wouldn't accept my order to stand down."

"And if I don't agree to accept it now?" she asked.

"Well then, I'll have to insist and put a few guards around Joel's house to keep the two of you from leaving. Do I need to do that, Trista?" he asked.

"No," she whispered. The last thing that either of them needed was to feel trapped in his house. She had a feeling that Joel wouldn't go for that at all. He had already snuck out to go for a run while she was sleeping. "That won't be necessary."

"So, you'll accept my order and stand down?" Henry asked.

Trista sighed, "I will," she agreed, "reluctantly."

"Noted," Henry said. "You two stay put, and I'll keep you as informed as I possibly can, under the circumstances." Trista wouldn't rely on her boss to keep her up to date on the Gemini case. She had a few friends in the bureau who would help with that. She was sure that Henry wouldn't give her the information that she needed anyway.

"I appreciate that," Trista said, trying to keep the peace. "Talk soon," she said, ending the call. She tossed her cell phone to the couch and turned to find Joel standing in the doorway.

"Everything good?" he asked.

"No," she mumbled. Joel crossed the room to where she stood and reached out to take her hand into his own.

"Want to talk about it?" he asked.

"No," she breathed, "I've been kicked off of the Gemini Brother's case because my boss thinks I'm too close to it. I mean, maybe I am, since Dante killed my little brother, but to be kicked off the case hurts, you know?" she asked.

"I've been kicked off a few cases over the years, and I have to admit, it does suck. But we'll find a way to get through all of this, Trista. We've both been removed from this case, and neither of us is about to back down from it, so we'll figure it out."

"Thanks for saying that, Joel," she said.

He nodded, "I've got breakfast ready if you're hungry."

"Sounds great," Trista, "thanks for being so good about everything, Joel." She followed him into the kitchen and sat in the chair that he had pulled out for her. He was being so nice to her, that she wasn't sure if she wanted to cry or laugh. For now, she'd settle for breakfast, and then, she'd call a few of her contacts to find out where Dante went to.

JOEL

THEY ATE THEIR BREAKFAST MAKING SMALL TALK, BUT ALL JOEL wanted to do was talk with her about that scorching kiss that they shared, but he could tell that Trista wasn't ready to talk about any of it. In fact, he could tell that she was going to avoid talking about the kiss that they shared at all.

She sighed and pushed her half-full plate back from her place at the table. "You know, we're going to have to talk about it, right?" she asked.

"Okay," he agreed, "you go first." He was relieved that they were going to put the topic of their kiss behind them so that he could discuss the possibility of more kissing in the future.

"Fine, I don't think that it's safe for you to leave the house and go for runs on your own. Do you have someone you can run with?" she asked.

"What?" he asked. Was she really going to discuss him going for a jog this morning over their hot kiss in that very kitchen?

"You can't just go out by yourself, Joel," she repeated. "What if Dante has his men scoping this place out? You could have been taken or worse. You really need a jogging partner."

"You're talking about me going jogging?" he asked, trying to keep up.

"Are you all right?" she asked. "I feel like you were expecting us to talk about something else."

"I was," he admitted. "I mean, I thought that we were going to talk about our kiss."

"Our kiss?" she asked. Now, she seemed to be the one trying to keep up with their conversation.

"Yeah—that hot as hell kiss that you gave me before your boss called you," he reminded.

"I remember the kiss, Joel, but I don't think that there really is anything to discuss about it. It was a kiss, nothing more," she insisted. It was so much more than a kiss and she knew it too. He could see the truth written all over her face.

"Just a kiss?" he asked.

"Yes, Joel," she said, "it was just a kiss. Please don't tell me that was the first time that you've ever kissed a girl, Joel," she teased.

"No, it's not the first time I've kissed a woman, Trista," he insisted. "You told me that you know that Melody and I were together."

"Yes, I know about you and Melody," she said.

"Then, I'm sure that you can guess that I've kissed a woman at least once," he said.

"You know, this is really the most ridiculous conversation that I've ever had with another person," Trista said.

"We could go back to talking about me going jogging. How about you go with me?" he asked. "That way, I'll be following the rule of no jogging alone."

"I don't run—not unless I'm chasing someone or being chased."

"Well, I'll chase you, if it helps," he teased.

"Ha, ha," Trista drawled, "I'm not going running with you. I did notice that you have a treadmill in the basement and some weights. Why not use that instead of putting your life at risk to run outside?" she asked.

"You were in my basement?" he questioned.

"Yes, I was looking for the bodies that you must have hidden down there," Trista joked. The more he talked to her, the more Joel liked Trista. She was not only beautiful, but she was funny too.

"You're funny," he said. "I missed that last night while you had a gun pointed at me. But you're really funny, Trista," she said.

"Thanks," she said, "my brother used to say that to me all the time. I guess I haven't had much to be funny about lately. You know, since he's been gone."

"Yeah, I guess that could take the fun out of life—losing a sibling like that. How have your parents held up, losing their son?"

"Not well," she admitted. "I don't go over there as much as I should because I really hate seeing them that way. They seem to just be going through the motions in life, just surviving day to day. It's painful to see."

"I bet it would be hard to watch. Were you all close before your brother died?" he asked.

"Yes, before Pete died, we used to have Sunday dinner every week, and mom and dad would tell us that they weren't getting any younger and they'd try to guilt us into giving them, grandchildren. Of course, Pete and I would explain to them that we'd need to meet someone to do that and that we were both committed to our jobs. They'd get angry and tell us that we just didn't care about them, and we'd end up having a heated debate about our dating lives. You know, before I would have told you that I hated all of it, but now, I have to admit, I miss it."

"I'm sorry," Joel said.

"Thanks but talking about Pete helps. At first, I couldn't even say his name, but now that some time has passed, it's gotten easier," she admitted. "I just don't ever want to forget him, you know?"

"I'm sure that you won't forget your brother," Joel assured. She nodded and he could tell that she was ready to change the subject. "If you're off the case, how will we get updates about Dante?"

"I have some contacts in the CIA who will keep me in the loop, even if I'm not on the case. Plus, my boss has already given me a pretty big clue to go off of. He said that his intel has Dante in another location. He moved his operation and that's probably why we haven't been able to trace him down since his release."

"Yeah, that helps," Joel agreed. "How about you track down your contacts and I'll do the same? I'm betting that we'll be able to track him down in no time if we combine forces."

"I agree," she said. "I'll be up in my room if you don't mind." She stood and turned back to him. "By the way, you were right about your mattress—it was awful."

"Just say the word and I'll trade with you," he offered.

"No, I'll be fine," she lied. He wanted to offer to let her crawl into his bed with him, but he was sure that one kiss didn't warrant such an offer.

Joel woke in the middle of the night and realized that the downstairs lights were on. He must have left them on before going up to bed. He threw off his covers, noting the chill in the air, and pulled on his sweatpants. He passed Trista's closed door and thought about peeking in to make sure that she was all right but decided against it. If she was sleeping, he didn't want to wake her.

He walked down the steps and found the family room light in the corner on, and as he walked across the room to turn it off, he found Trista sound asleep on his sofa, covered with a thin quilt that he kept on the sofa. She had to be freezing and he hated that she was on his very lumpy sofa, trying to get some rest.

"Trista," he whispered, "Trista, honey." She moaned and rolled over, almost falling onto the floor. "Careful," he said, crossing the room to sit down next to her on the sofa so that she wouldn't fall off.

"What's going on?" she mumbled.

"I noticed that the light was on and came down to find you," he said.

"Oh, sorry, I must have left the light on by accident," she breathed.

"I'm not upset about the light," he admitted, "but I'm worried that you're on the sofa. What's wrong?"

"The bed in your guest room is awful," she said. "The sofa is a bit better, and I just need to get some sleep."

"Well, you can't sleep down here," Joel said, "you'll freeze to death."

"I can't go back to my room," she said, "in the morning, I'm going to order a new mattress for your guest room."

"No," he said, "I'll buy the mattress. I'm sorry that I didn't replace it sooner. I had plans to do so, but I don't get many overnight guests."

"Listen, you should go back to bed," she insisted. "I'll be fine here for the night."

"No, you won't be," Joel insisted. He held out his hand to her and she looked at him as if he had lost his mind. "Come on," he said.

"Come on where?" she asked.

"Just come with me," he said, "you can have half of my bed."

"Half of your bed," she repeated, "will you be in the other half?"

"I will be," he admitted, "is that a problem?"

"I'm not sure," she said, "will you be staying on your side of the bed all night?" she asked.

"If that's what you want, Trista," he said.

"What if I want you to slide over to my side of the bed during the night?" she asked. He got hard just hearing her ask him to slide over to her side of the bed.

"Don't tease me," he insisted, "I'm already on edge when it comes to you, Trista," he admitted.

"On edge how?" she asked, "I mean, what have I done to you, Joel?" He was willing to forget that she had held him at gunpoint. She was trying to save him and do the right thing. But since she had moved into his place, Trista had gotten under his skin on more than a few occasions.

"One minute, you're kissing me, and the next, you're pushing me away," he said. "I'm having trouble keeping up with it all, and now, you're asking me if I'll slide over to your side of the bed during the night."

"I didn't mean to upset you," she grumbled, "I was just hoping that you'd want, well—more."

"More?" he asked, "What are we talking about here, Trista?" he asked.

"Sex, Joel," she spat, "I'm talking about sex and I'm tired of playing games. Hell, I'm just plain tired, and if I don't get some sleep soon, I really won't care where I end up sleeping."

"I'd like more with you, Trista," he agreed, "I'd like sex."

She giggled, "Most men do," Trista teased.

"Ha, ha," he mumbled. Joel held out his hand to her again and this time, she smiled up at him and took it. "Thank you for not fighting me on this," he said.

"Do you usually expect a fight from me, Joel?" she asked.

"Yes," he admitted, "I usually expect a fight with you. I swear, Trista, I say that the sky is blue, and you refute me, even telling me I'm wrong."

"Well, you make it easy, Joel," she said, "you do come up with some pretty crazy ideas." She was right, he did. "I just find it easy to fight with you for some reason."

"I'll try to give you fewer reasons to fight with me from here on out, Trista," he said, leading her into his bedroom. "Do you have a side of the bed that you prefer?" he asked.

"Um, the middle," she said.

Joel chuckled, "Well then, I can't promise to stay on my side of the bed."

"I really don't care which side of the bed that I sleep on, as long as it's not lumpy and doesn't have a spring poking me in the ass every time I roll over."

"Is that what happened in the guest room?" he asked.

"Yes, your bed violated me hourly. I'm just hoping that your mattress in here is better," she said.

"It is," he assured. Joel felt like an ass for sticking her in the spare room and not giving her his bed from the start.

"Make yourself at home," he said, nodding to the bed. He watched as she climbed into his bed, crawling under the covers, and damn if she didn't look right there.

"Good?" he asked.

"Yes," she agreed, "your bed is very comfy." Joel crawled into bed next to her and got under the covers. He felt her leg brush his and she apologized.

"We're bound to collide," he said, "you can't apologize every time we touch," he insisted.

"I'll try not to," she said, "it's a habit. I've been raised to be polite."

"You don't need to be polite around me," he promised. "In fact, I can think of a few ways that I'd like you to be very impolite with me." Trista's gasp filled the room, and he knew he should have regretted what he just said to her, but he didn't. He couldn't because he wanted her more than he wanted his next breath.

TRISTA

Trista wasn't sure that she had heard Joel correctly at first, but when she realized that she had, she couldn't help her gasp. "Joel," she whispered. He couldn't be serious. They had only just met, and she held him at gunpoint. "You can't be serious."

"But I am," he insisted. He rolled over and wrapped an arm around her waist.

"You are breaking your rule about staying on your side of the bed," she said.

"Do you want me to go back to my side?" Joel asked. He was challenging her, testing her to see how she'd react to him touching her. He had already kissed her, and she liked that. Hell, she more than liked it, but that didn't mean that the two of them should sleep together. How would that even work?

"No," she breathed, giving him the truth. "I don't want you to go back to your side of the bed, Joel." Trista put her leg over his, effectively trapping him in place. "I'd like for you to stay right here."

"All right," he breathed, "I think that can be arranged. So, if I stay here, what happens next?" he asked.

Trista knew just what she wanted to happen next—she just needed to be bold enough to ask him for it. "This should happen next," she said, leaning in to brush her lips over his. When she pulled back from him, Joel was smiling like a loon.

"Then what?" he asked.

"How about this?" Trista asked, sliding her hands down his abs and dipping them into his sweatpants. "No boxers?" she asked.

"Well, I was sleeping naked, but I thought that walking downstairs that way might not be a good thing, since you're my houseguest." She ran her hands over his erection and Joel hissed out his breath.

"I wouldn't have minded you coming downstairs naked," she insisted. "Does this feel good?" she asked, running her fingers over the head of his cock.

"Yes," he breathed. "It feels fantastic. Don't stop."

"But then, we wouldn't be able to do this next," she said, pulling her hands free from his sweats and climbing on top of him. She straddled his erection and rubbed herself over his sweats.

"Oh, I like this too," he whispered as she dipped her head

to kiss him. "But I think that we're both wearing too many clothes."

"I agreed," she said. He watched her as she tugged her t-shirt up over her head, leaving her in just her shorts. His hands ran up her tummy to her breasts as he played with her nipples.

"That feels good," she whimpered.

"How about this?" Joel asked, as he ran his hands back down her body and dipped them into her shorts. Trista hissed out her breath and Joel chuckled. "Turnabout's fair play, honey," he teased. He ran his fingers through her wet folds, and she nearly bucked off of his bed. It had been so long since any man had touched her that way. Trista had gotten used to taking care of her own needs, she had forgotten what it felt like to have a man touch her there.

"You're already so wet for me," Joel whispered into her ear as she leaned against his body.

"I need more," she insisted, "please, Joel."

"I'll take good care of you, honey," he promised, "I just want to make sure that you're ready for me."

"I'm more than ready," she practically growled. Joel laughed again and she shot him a look.

"Not funny," she breathed.

"I'm sorry," he said, pulling her down on top of his body. "Are you sure that you're ready?"

"Yes," she insisted.

"Are you always so impatient?" he asked.

"When it comes to sex, yes," she admitted. "It's been a long time since I've been with a man, I guess I'm anxious." That was an understatement. She was downright impatient at the thought of him taking her.

"I won't make you wait any longer than necessary," he promised.

"How can you say that when you're still wearing clothes?" she asked.

"You're right," he said, "I think that first, we need to get rid of these." He tugged down her shorts, palming her bare ass as he tried to work them down her legs. Joel rolled her underneath his body and finished shimming them down her legs, leaving her completely bare. When he finished stripping her, he pulled his sweatpants off, letting his cock spring free between them. Trista couldn't help herself. Her hands went directly to his shaft, and Joel hummed his approval.

"You keep playing with me like that and this will be over before I even get in you, honey," he said.

"Well, we don't want that," she insisted. Joel pulled her back on top of his body and she loved the idea of being in charge. Trista loved to be on top.

"You're letting me be on top?" she asked.

"Is that okay?" he asked.

"It's more than okay," Trista said, "I like a bit of control," she admitted.

"Take all the control that you want, honey," he said, holding his arms wide. Trista took that as her invitation to climb on top of Joel and take what her body was screaming at her to take. She lined up his cock with her wet folds and let him slide inside of her body. When she fully seated herself on him, they both groaned out loud and she was pretty sure that Joel was the sexiest man that she'd ever seen.

Trista braced herself, putting her hands on his pecks, as she rode his cock, taking what she needed from him, and when she cried out that she was going to come, Joel told her to do it. Hearing him coaxing her to come for him was all she needed and when she called out his name, Joel shouted out hers too, finding his own release. She collapsed on top of him as he wrapped his arms protectively around her.

"Stay in my room with me," he said.

"I'll stay all night," Trista promised.

"That's not what I meant, honey," he breathed. "I want you to stay in my bed with me from now on. Move in here with me."

"Permanently?" she asked. "You want me to sleep in here every night?"

"Yes," he admitted, "I want you in my bed every night. Are you good with that?" he asked.

"I am," she agreed. Trista was more than okay with the idea of crawling into bed with him every night that she was there with him—no matter how long that turned out to be.

Trista moved into Joel's room the next morning, as promised, and she was about to jump into the shower when Joel came running into the bedroom. "Melody has called, and we have a lead on Dante," he said. He was out of breath as if he had just run a race and all she could think about was last night—the way that he panted out her name when he came, sweaty and out of breath.

"Well, that's good news," she said, trying to keep her mind out of the gutter. "Where is he and how soon can we move in?" she asked.

"He's in a small warehouse across town, and Melody is calling the team together now. You up for a raid?" he asked. "I know that I've been kicked off the case, but I still need to call this into Henry," she insisted. Trista was still an agent and had to do things by the book. It was just who she was.

"Do you think that's a good idea?" he asked. "I mean, Henry did kick you off of the case, to begin with. I'd be happy to make you one of my officers for the time being."

She giggled, "I can't be one of your officers, but I'd bet you'd love to boss me around."

"I would love to boss you around, honey, but we can save that for later. Do what you have to do, and I'll get the team ready. I'd love for you to come along with us," he said.

"I wouldn't miss it for anything," she said. "I want to bring Dante in as much as you do, Joel, probably more. He killed my brother."

"I remember," he said, "and I'll do whatever I can to help

you bring down the Gemini Brothers to avenge your brother's death, Trista."

"Thank you," she said. "I appreciate you saying that, Joel." It felt good to have a partner again. She had been working solo for so long, that she almost forgot what that felt like. It was nice knowing that Joel would have her back, no matter what this case brought on.

JOEL

THEY HAD BEEN ON TWO RAIDS, AND BOTH TURNED OUT TO BE busts. Melody had good intel, but somehow, Dante Gemini was staying one step ahead of them the whole time. It almost felt as though someone was ratting them out, and warning Dante that they were on their way to raid his warehouse. The one thing that they knew for certain, was he didn't have any women yet because there was no sign of them being moved. In fact, the last place that they checked out had no cages and nowhere for Dante to store his human cargo.

The only good thing about them not catching up with Dante was that Trista had to stay with him a bit longer. He loved having her at his place, but he could tell that she was still a bit hesitant about what was happening between the two of them. He'd just have to make good use of his time and get her to see the benefits of living with him.

Joel found Trista in the kitchen, making herself a cup of tea and he smiled and pulled down a mug for himself. "Do you mind if I join you?" he asked.

"Not at all," she said, putting a teabag into his cup. "Sugar?" she asked.

"Please," he said.

"Any news from Melody this morning?" she asked. He had let Trista sleep in while he worked out in the basement this morning. She seemed to be tired lately, and he hated that he might be demanding too much of her at night. The problem was, he just couldn't seem to keep his hands to himself when Trista was around.

"No," he said, "it has been quiet—too quiet."

"Well, it gave me time to catch up on my sleep," she breathed.

"Yeah, I'm sorry about keeping you up half the night," he said.

"Don't be," she insisted, "I like that you want me, Joel."

"Oh honey, I want you," he admitted, "there should be no doubt about that." Trista wrapped her arms around his neck and gently kissed his lips. Every time she kissed him like that, he wanted to take more from her.

The kettle started to whistle, and Joel moved it from the burner. "The tea can wait."

"It can?" she asked.

"Yeah, first, I'd like to discuss you getting naked with me," he said.

"You would?" she asked. "And after I get naked, what

would you like me to do?" she asked, running her hands down his body to cup his erection through his boxers.

"I want you to get down on those pretty little knees of yours and well, I'm sure you can figure it out from there, honey."

"I really like the way you think, Joel," she said. Trista stripped and pulled his boxers down his body, letting them fall around his ankles as she got on her knees in front of him. She ran her hands over his cock and when she licked the head, he hissed out his breath.

"Don't play with me, Trista," he ordered. She giggled and sucked him into her warm mouth, to the back of her throat, letting Joel hold himself there. He was careful not to gag her too badly, pulling free from her lips to let her catch her breath.

"You are so fucking perfect," he rasped.

"Hey guys," Melody said, walking in through the back door.

"Shit," Joel shouted, "out, Melody," he yelled.

"Oh my God," Melody squealed. "In the fucking kitchen, Joel? I'm so sorry, Trista," she said, "I'll, um, I'll be outside."

Trista sat on the floor in front of him, trying to cover herself with her arms and legs, but failing miserably. "She's gone," he said. Joel pulled his boxers up and helped Trista up from the floor. "I'm so sorry," he said, pulling her into his arms. "Get dressed, and I'll find out what Melody wants."

"But you're in your underwear," Trista reminded.

"Right, I'll put on some pants and a t-shirt, and then, I'll go talk to her. We need to set up rules for her just walking in."

"Yeah, we do," Trista agreed. "And maybe, we should lock the back door if we're going to have sex in the kitchen again." It was good to hear her say that they were going to actually try this again.

"Right," he agreed. "I'll talk to her about knocking and we'll lock the doors from now on."

"All right," Trista said. "When she's gone, come find me in the shower. I think that I'd like to finish what we just started."

"Now, that sounds like a good plan, honey," he agreed. "I won't be long."

"See you soon," she promised. Joel grabbed some clean clothes that he had folded out of the laundry basket and pulled them on. He was going to deal with Melody, and then, he was going to find his girl and finish what they had just started. As far as mornings went, this one might have started off crazy, but he planned on a happy ending—one way or another.

They were having dinner when the front doorbell rang, and Joel nearly choked on his steak. "Who the hell could that be?" Trista asked. When Savage or Melody stopped by to bring them provisions, or just check on them, they just came in through the back door. Of course, they always called or texted to let them know that they were on their way. Melody liked to joke that walking in on the two of them naked wasn't her idea of a good time. Sure, that had happened once, and Joel learned an important lesson to lock the back door before having sex with Trista in the kitchen, but his partner should have known not to just barge into his home.

Trista got up from the table and grabbed her gun from the kitchen counter. "I've got it," she insisted.

"Um, I think that we can at least check to see who it is first before we show up guns blazing," Joel teased.

"No one rings the bell, Joel," she insisted. "This feels like a setup." It did, and she was right, but he wasn't about to tell her that and make her worry even more. They made a good team—he was the optimist, and she was the pessimist in the relationship, and that worked for them.

"Right, and that's why I'm going to answer the door," he insisted.

The bell rang again, and Trista rolled her eyes at him. "We can stand here and argue about all of this, or we can just agree to answer the door together."

"Fine, but if this goes south, I want you behind me," Joel ordered.

"If this goes south, I'm betting that we'll both be dead," Trista corrected. She followed him to the front door and no matter how many times he tried to shove her behind his body, she got to the door first and pulled it open, gun pointed at the guy standing on his porch.

Joel stepped in front of her and stared the guy down, "Can I help you?" he asked.

"I'd like to speak to my sister," the man said.

"I think that you have the wrong address," Joel insisted. "I live here alone, and I'm pretty sure that your sister isn't here."

"She's standing right behind you," the man said, nodding to Trista. Her gasp filled the entryway and Joel stepped aside as she tried to shove him out of the way.

"Peter," she breathed. "Is it really you?"

"Surprise," the guy said, waving his hands in the air as if he had just jumped out at the guest of honor at a birthday party. "It's really me."

"Trista," Joel said, putting his hand on her shoulder, "are you all right?"

"No," she breathed, "I'm not all right. My dead brother is standing on your porch." Joel looked the guy over, "He doesn't look dead to me," he said. "You want to tell us what's going on here, man?" Joel asked. Trista laid her gun on the table that he had by his front door.

"I'd like to handle this, Joel," Trista insisted.

"Are you sure?" he asked. She didn't look to be sure about anything, but he wanted to give her time with her brother if that's what she wanted.

"I'm sure," Trista whispered.

TRISTA

Trista walked out to the porch where her brother was standing. She looked him over as if trying to find some clue that he wasn't who he claimed to be. "Do you want me to come out with you, honey?" Joel asked.

"No," she whispered, "I've got this. I need to talk to him alone." She turned back just in time to see the hurt on Joel's face and that wasn't her intent, but she'd have to fix that later. Right now, she wanted to figure out if the man standing next to her was really Peter.

"You're dead," she breathed.

He held out his hands and spun around, "Do I look dead to you, Sis?" he asked.

"No," she said. "You look very much alive which leads me to my next question—why did you allow me to believe that you were dead this whole time? We had a funeral for you and everything. The Gemini Brothers shipped your body back in pieces to our parents. Do you know what that did to them?"

"That's more than one question," Pete teased.

"Don't joke about this, Peter," she insisted. "Mom almost had a nervous breakdown and Dad hasn't been the same since the day they lowered your coffin into the ground. If that wasn't you in the coffin, who was it?"

Pete shrugged, "Don't really know who was in my coffin. It wasn't me though."

"I think that I'm going to need a bit more of an explanation than you don't know who was buried in your place, Pete. What the hell is going on?"

"Can I come in and we can talk?" he asked. "I think that Joel should be a part of the conversation too, since he's the one who has kept you safe this whole time, Sis."

"How do I know that I can trust you?" she asked. "How do I know that you're not working for Dante Gemini like he says you were?" Dante had told the CIA agent, who questioned him after he was first arrested, that Peter was a double agent. He convinced the agent that Pete was working for him. Trista had actually started to believe that her brother had double-crossed them all when pieces of his body started showing up. Why would Dante Gemini murder someone whom he claimed double-crossed the CIA for him? He wouldn't, so Trista refused to believe his stories. Instead, she helped her parents bury her brother and was trying to move on. Until now, when she found her dead brother standing on Joel's porch.

"Ahh, Dante told you that I was working for him," he said. She nodded her head and he sighed. "Well, that's actually good news. It's just what I wanted him to believe. It's why I had to stage my death. I'm sorry about upsetting Mom and Dad, but I had to do that to keep both of them and you safe."

"Safe," she spat, "how exactly do you think you've kept us safe? You put our whole family on Dante's radar, and he won't stop until we're all dead. Mom and Dad are both in protective custody and Joel and I have been laying low while trying, and failing I might add, to bring down Dante's trafficking ring."

"I think that I can help with that," Peter promised. "Please, just let me in so that I can explain everything from the beginning."

Trista looked back at Joel, and he nodded. "It wouldn't hurt to just hear him out, honey," he said. She hated that he was right, but he was.

"Fine," she said, "you can come in, but if I think that you're lying to me, Pete, I'm tossing you out."

"Got it," he agreed. He walked past her and followed Joel into his house. They made their way to the kitchen, and she was sure that inviting her brother in was a big mistake. How was she ever going to tell her parents about their son lying to them? He deliberately hurt them all, and now, she was going to have to break that news to them.

"Sit and spill it," Trista ordered, "and, start from the beginning."

"Still as bossy as ever," Peter teased. He sat at the end of the table and she and Joel sat at the other end. "I missed you, Sis," he admitted.

"Well, if that was true, you would have found a way to tell me that you were alive," she shouted.

"Right, but that would have put you all in danger," Pete said.

"Yeah, you've already said that," Trista reminded.

"Well, it bears repeating," Pete said. "Everything that I did, I did it for my family—to keep you all safe."

She nodded and waved her hands through the air. "Can you just get on with what happened, please?" Trista asked.

"I've been deep undercover on the Gemini case," he said. "My mission was classified, and you didn't have clearance to be in the know."

"Bullshit," Trista shouted. "I have top clearance. I have more clearance than you, Pete," she said.

"Yeah, but this was top secret. I wasn't allowed to talk about it to anyone, including you, Sis. God, I wanted to. I tried to convince the powers that be to let me confide in you. I didn't want you or our parents to suffer because of me. I was turned down and told that you knowing—"

"Would put us all in danger," she filled in for him.

"Right, so I went along with the plan and followed orders. I knew that I had to do whatever I could to bring down Dante and his trafficking ring," Pete said. "But then, every-thing went sideways, and your new boyfriend here stormed in and arrested Dante. I was made, and I thought for sure that I was dead."

"I was told that the Gemini Brothers figured out that you were an agent and that's when they made an example out of you and murdered you," Trista said.

"Yeah, that's what the CIA wanted you to believe. They were the ones who got me out just before the Gemini brothers could make good on their threats. When they found out that I was an agent, they put me in a cell, telling me that they were going to hold me to let Dante deal with me. None of the other guys wanted to have my blood on their hands. They knew that killing an agent would land them on death row. Plus, it would piss Dante off if he didn't get to kill me himself, once he made bail, so they left me in that cell to rot."

"That's awful, man," Joel said.

"Yeah, it wasn't very much fun, that's for sure, but I was happy to just be alive, you know?" Pete asked.

"I get it," Joel said.

"As you both know, Dante never got out. You all had enough on him to hold him, but that really didn't help me at all. I was afraid that I'd end up dying in that cage if no one found me."

"What happened?" Trista asked. "How did you get out?"

"My team came in and got me out of there," Pete said. "It wasn't easy. We barely made it out of there alive, and when I got back to the bureau, I was pulled into a room and told that as far as anyone else was concerned, I was dead. I tried to argue that I couldn't let my family believe that I was dead, but they vetoed my opinion and told me their plan on how they were going to make everyone believe that I was dead.

I'm guessing that's where the body parts that they sent home to be buried as me, came into play. I'm not sure how it all worked, I didn't ask many questions at that point. All I knew was that I was dead. It was what Dante and the Gemini Brothers needed to believe, and I really didn't ask questions. The agency put me up in a safe house and I stayed there until you two got Dante released."

"Yeah, we've been trying to get the evidence that we need to bring down his entire organization, but he's been able to stay one step ahead of us," Joel admitted.

"I didn't know that the local authorities had anything to do with the Gemini Brothers or their trafficking ring," Pete said.

"Don't be mean, Pete," Trista insisted.

"Was I being mean?" Pete asked. He knew exactly what he was doing. He wanted to get back at Joel for putting him in the position that he had. "He had no idea what was going on in the CIA. He never got the message to stand down. Joel isn't the one to blame for all of this."

"Who is to blame then?" Peter asked.

"The Gemini Brothers," Trista said, "and that's why Joel and I are working together now."

"Does the agency know that you two are working together?" Pete asked.

"Well, that's none of your business," Trista said.

"It is my business, Sis," he insisted. "This is still my case." She had been off the case since she and Joel had to disappear. The agency didn't want her drawing attention to her or Joel, so they removed her from the Gemini case. It was a slap in the face, and her boss knew it, but there was no way that he'd let her come back as long as Dante was still out there.

"They don't have any idea that we're still working the case," Joel said.

"Joel," Trista shouted, "do you have to be so honest all the damn time?" she asked.

He flashed her his sexy smile, and he knew exactly what that did to her. Joel wasn't playing fair, and he didn't seem to care.

"Listen, I don't know what to say or not say here, but I believe your brother," he admitted.

"Well, you shouldn't say that," Trista insisted.

"Hey," Pete said, "why not? I mean, if he's just sharing his opinion, what does it hurt?"

"Because I haven't decided if I believe you yet, Pete," she said. "I just need some time to think about everything."

"I get it," Pete said. "I need you to keep my secret," he said. "You can't tell Mom and Dad yet."

"I'm not allowed to tell our parents that their only son is still alive?" Trista asked.

"No, he said. I'm back in Dante's good graces and he thinks that I'm a double agent. I need for him to believe that I'm double-crossing the CIA and working for him now," Pete said.

"How did you get back into the Gemini Brothers if they know that you're an agent?" Joel asked.

"Because I helped him to escape the last time the CIA was

going to raid his warehouse. I convinced him that I wanted out of the agency, and when I told him about the raid, he started to trust me again."

"So, you're the reason why we can't catch a break in the case," Trista said.

He shrugged, "Probably," Pete admitted. "You were going to raid an empty warehouse and that would only end with Dante getting out of jail again. He's keeping them all just across state lines. So, that will mean that you're out," he said, pointing at Joel.

"Shit," Joel growled.

"I know that we need to bring down his whole organization, and to do that, we need to raid his new warehouse," Pete said. "I just need more time, and then you can move in," he said to Trista.

"I'm not on the case anymore," she spat, "remember?"

"Right, but I plan on changing that. You know about me now, so there's no reason to keep you in the dark about the Gemini Brothers. Are you in or out, Sis?" he asked.

She sighed, already knowing what her answer was going to be.

"I'm in," she said, "but, only if I can have Joel on my team. I know that this doesn't fall under local jurisdiction, but I trust him and don't want anyone else watching my back."

"I think that can be arranged," Pete agreed.

"How much time will you need?" Joel asked.

"Three to four days," Pete said. "Dante's got a shipment of women coming in over the weekend. We need him to have a full house so that we can put him away for the rest of his life. The more women he has in cages, the longer his sentence will be."

"Those poor women," Trista breathed.

"Are you up for this, Sis?" Pete asked. That was a good question. Every time she raided a warehouse full of women, she felt sick. She was saving them, but would they be able to go back to their lives after what they had already endured? Most of the women had already been raped or beaten for not complying. Hell, sometimes they were beaten up for the sport of it. The men who took them and put them into cages didn't care about how those women felt or who they were before they were taken. They might never be able to reintegrate back into their lives, and that thought made Trista sad, but it didn't mean that she'd give up helping them.

"I'm up for it," she said. "You don't need to worry about me, Pete," she assured.

"Good," Pete said, "I'll be in touch just as soon as the women are in place. In the meantime, you two should continue to lay low and don't tell anyone about our meeting. As far as anyone else is concerned, I'm still a dead man." Trista nodded, knowing that keeping this secret from her parents was going to be tough. Maybe not calling her mother and father for the next week might be the best plan. She wasn't very good at keeping secrets from either of them, and Pete being alive was one doozy of a secret to have to keep.

"Got it," she agreed. "Just don't keep us waiting too long,"

Trista ordered. "And Pete—be careful. I don't want to have to bury you again."

"I'll try not to die again," he teased, kissing her cheek. "It was good to see you, Sis," he said, "and, it was good to meet you, Joel."

"You too, man," Joel said, "and for the record, I'm glad that you're not dead."

"Me too, man, me too," Pete said. Trista walked him out to his truck and watched him drive off until she could no longer see his taillights in the distance.

"You okay?" Joel asked, wrapping his arms around her from behind.

"No, but I will be," she whispered. "I just need some time to process that my brother is still alive."

"Take all the time you need, honey," Joel said. "I'm going to make us some dinner and then, how about we take a walk in the woods?" he asked. Trista loved that his property backed to woods that went on for miles behind his cabin. Their evening walks through the woods were her favorite time of day.

"I'd love that," she agreed, "thank you for being here for me, Joel," she said.

"Anytime, honey," he agreed, "anytime."

JOEL

JOEL WORRIED THAT TRISTA'S BROTHER SHOWING BACK UP from the dead might throw a kink in their plans—and it did. She had all but backed down from secretly working the case with him. He wanted to bring Dante down, but Pete was right, if they could just be patient and wait for the Gemini Brothers to "restock" they'd be able to put him away for life as well as bring down the whole organization. The only problem that Joel had with the plan was that he wasn't a patient man.

Trista seemed to retreat into herself, not really coming out of their room much. Ever since she moved into his master bedroom, after their first night together, he had considered it to be "their room." He just hoped that Trista was beginning to feel that way too because when this nightmare was over, he was going to ask her to move in with him.

Joel found Trista sitting in the kitchen, having a cup of coffee, and staring off into space. "You okay?" he asked. He could see the answer on her face—she wasn't.

"Will he ever call?" she asked. It had been almost two months since Peter had turned up from the land of the dead, and he promised to call them as soon as he was ready to have them move in on Dante's warehouse, but that was supposed to happen over a month ago.

Pete had stayed true to his word and got Trista back on the Gemini Brother's case. She was told that she was being taken off the case because she was too close to it. Her boss, Henry, told her that he wanted to take her off of the Gemini case as soon as Pete died, but he gave her some time. What he failed to tell her was that he knew that Pete was alive the whole time. Her boss was in on the plan to keep Pete under-cover in the Gemini Brothers, and he never told her. When Trista found that out, she was pissed, but she let it go when Henry promised to put her back on the case. She was in charge of the team that would go in when Pete gave the go-ahead.

The problem was that the last time that they heard from Pete was almost two weeks ago. Her brother was supposed to check in every three days, but it had been almost two weeks since he last checked in and Trista was worried. If he was being honest, he was worried about Pete too, but he kept that to himself.

"You just have to be patient," he assured. "I'm sure that he'll check in as soon as he can do so safely."

"So, you believe he's in danger then?" she asked.

"That's not what I said, honey," Joel said. "I just think that he's been busy and doesn't want to blow his cover."

"Which is it?" Trista asked. "Is he too busy to call to tell us that he's all right, or is he worried that calling us will blow his cover?" He had no idea, really. He was just trying to ease her mind, but Trista wasn't looking for that. No, his girl was looking for a fight and he wasn't about to give her one.

"I won't fight with you, honey," he said.

"Why the hell not?" she spat. "It would make me feel better."

"So would a spanking," he teased. She stood from her chair and turned to look him over. He was sure that what he had said pissed her off, but from the need that he saw in her eyes, he was wrong. "You'd like that?" he asked.

"Yes," she almost whispered. "I like to be spanked."

"We've been together for over two months now and you never told me that you like to be spanked?" he asked.

"We're still so new to each other, and well, I didn't want to scare you off or have you think of me as a freak if it was something that you weren't into."

"Oh, I'm into it," he insisted. He was more than into it. He loved a little bit of kink when it came to sex, but he was too afraid to bring it up to Trista. "I was also too afraid to bring it up so early in our relationship."

"Is that what we're doing here, Joel?" she asked. "We're having a relationship?"

"I'd like to think so if you're good with that," he said.

89

"I am," he agreed, "I like to think of you as my girlfriend. In fact, when I was talking to Axel the other day, when he checked in on us, I called you my girlfriend and he gave me a bunch of shit."

She snuggled in against his body and Joel wrapped his arms around her, tugging her close. "Well, I for one like it when you call me your girlfriend," she insisted.

"Good to know," he whispered, dipping his head to kiss her lips. God, he couldn't wait to get his hands on her ass. "Can I spank you, honey?" he asked.

"I'd like that," she agreed. He wasn't one to usually ask, but things between them were still so new, he wanted to make sure that she was on board for everything that he wanted from her. "I'd like that, a lot," she added.

"Good, bend over the table," he said, "I'll lock the door."

Trista laughed, "Yeah, I don't think that I'd like Melody walking in to find you spanking me."

"No, this is just for us," he agreed. "Arms up," he ordered. Joel pulled her t-shirt up over her head, running his hands down her front, over her breasts, causing Trista to moan. He tugged down her shorts and ran his hands over her curvy ass. "Gorgeous," he breathed, kissing his way from her neck down her back. Joel wasted no time running his hand down her body and squeezing her ass into his big hand. He could feel how wet she was for him as he pulled his hand up and brought it down on her left globe. She moaned and thrust back against him as he rubbed the heat from her cheek.

"You good?" he asked.

"Yes," she hissed, "I need more." He was going to give her everything that she needed, but he also needed to make sure that she was with him every step of the way. She thrust back against his body and his cock seemed to spring to life. Joel wanted the spanking portion of their play to be over so that he could get inside of Trista, but he wouldn't rush her.

He peppered her ass with his hand, warming and marking both cheeks as she cried out his name. Joel knew that she was close and when he ran two fingers through her folds, feeling how wet she was for him, he couldn't help himself. He unzipped his jeans and let them fall to the kitchen floor he lined up his erection with her drenched opening and filled her with one thrust.

"You feel so good," he whispered into her ear from behind.

"You do too," she moaned. Every time he pulled almost completely out and shoved back into her body from behind, she cried out. "My ass is so sensitive." He knew exactly what he was doing to her, fucking her from behind after he just spanked her ass red. He pumped in and out of her body, and when Trista came, crying out his name, he knew that he wouldn't last much longer. He pressed her front down against the wooden table, holding her in place as he slammed into her body from behind. He wasn't gentle. Nothing about what he had just done to Trista was gentle, and she seemed to love every minute of it. She was perfect for him, and that very thought was what him coming into her body as he pumped into her from behind. He held her hips in place as he finished and when he was done, Joel pulled free from her body and flipped her over to face him.

"Are you all right?" he asked.

"I'm more than all right," she purred, wrapping her arms around his waist. "I'm great. Thank you for giving me what I needed, Joel," she said.

"Anytime," he whispered, gently kissing her lips. "I'll give you anything I possibly can, Trista," he promised. He wanted to tell her that he'd already given her his heart, but he was afraid that things were still too new for that admission. Instead, he lifted her into his arms and carried her up to his master bathroom. He was going to draw her a bath, and then, he was going to hope like hell that she'd allow him to join her. Holding Trista in a warm bath seemed like the perfect way to end their night. Tomorrow, they could worry about the rest of the world and what was going on with her brother. Tonight was for them—just the two of them.

Another week passed and Joel was sure that Trista was going to go out of her mind worrying about her brother. Her boss texted that he wanted her to come into the office and bring Joel, and he worried that they were going to be given bad news.

They quickly dressed and were in Henry's office within the hour. Trista was holding his hand so tight that he worried that she was going to stop his circulation.

"It's going to be all right," he assured, even if he didn't know that for certain.

"Hey guys, thanks for coming in so early," Henry said.

"No problem," Joel said, "what's the word?"

"Well, we've finally heard from Peter, and he's confirmed that Dante has taken a new shipment of women. They were delivered yesterday."

"Those poor women," Joel breathed.

"Where has Pete been? Why did it take him so long to get back to us?"

"There was a snag in the timeline and the women took an extra five weeks to round up. Apparently, Dante is having trust issues and he sent Peter out to do most of the dirty work. It took longer than he thought it would, but he assures me that Dante trusts him completely. He's practically become his second in command, and we need him in that position in order to take down the whole family." Hearing that things took longer than anticipated and that Pete was alive and well, should have put Trista's mind at ease, but it didn't seem to. Instead, Joel noticed that she was even more agitated at her boss's news.

"I'm not sure why he couldn't have at least called. I thought the worst for weeks," she said, trying to keep it together.

"I'm sorry, Trista," Henry said, "I've been worried about him too, but I can't imagine what you've been through these past few weeks. He told me that calling would have made

Dante suspicious. He said that his calls were being monitored."

"How did he finally call in?" Joel asked.

"He used one of the women's cell phones that they confiscated. He had to break into the office where they were locked away, but he got in touch and now, we're ready to move in. The rest of the questions can wait," Henry insisted. "All I need to know from both of you is that you're ready to get this investigation over with."

"My team is ready and willing to assist the CIA whenever you're ready, Henry," Joel promised.

"Good to hear," Henry said, "I really appreciate the assistance. I know that you have a personal interest in this case." He did. Joel was the arresting officer when Dante was brought in the first time. He had to lie and say that protocols weren't followed on his end when they released him. Now, he planned on being the one to put the cuffs back on Dante to bring him back in.

"I do," Joel said. "I appreciate you letting me be a part of this investigation."

Henry turned to look at Trista as if waiting out her answer. "I'm in," she agreed. "I might be pissed off at my brother, but I won't sit this one out. I want Dante back behind bars and now, he's going to have company. I can't wait to bring down his whole organization this time around."

"Good," Henry said. "We're meeting back here tonight at six. Have both of your teams here and ready to move. We'll go into the warehouse tonight. Dante plans on holding an auction tomorrow at noon and we'll need to bring down his organization before that happens."

Joel and Trista both stood and started out of the office. "This is going to work guys," Henry assured, "it has to. We have too much on the line for this mission to be anything but a success." Joel agreed with Trista's boss. They had to bring Dante back in—otherwise, they had released a monster into society and that was something that they couldn't let happen.

TRISTA

In the past couple of months, she and Joel had led their teams into two other warehouses, looking for Dante. Both times, they had come up empty, but that was because her brother was working behind the scenes to gain Dante's trust. He would tell him about the raids, having everything moved before they even got there and it was frustrating, to say the least.

Now, they were getting their chance to finally bring Dante in, and she wasn't sure what would happen after. She hoped that Joel would still want to be with her, but a part of her worried that he was just with her because of the danger that the case had put them both in. Joel said that he wanted her, but for how long?

And then, there was the whole matter of her brother.

They were going to have to come clean and tell her parents that they buried a body that wasn't their son. How would she ever explain that she had kept the secret that her brother was alive this whole time and she had known about it for months? There was no way that she'd expect her family to understand her keeping his secret because she didn't understand it. How could she keep something like that from her own parents?

After she found out about Pete, she thought about calling them to tell them about him being alive, but then, she'd remember that all of their safety depended on them not knowing. Plus, she was under strict orders from Henry not to tell anyone about Peter. It was the only way that he'd agree to bring her back on the Gemini Brother's case. It was a steep price to pay, but one that she was willing to because she wanted her chance to bring in Dante.

She and Joel called their team members to tell them to be ready to move in tonight. The whole mess was going to be over soon and driving into headquarters only made her realize that to be true. "You seem nervous," Joel whispered, pulling her hand into his own.

"I am," she admitted. "I guess everything's coming to an end and I'm just worried."

"Worried about what?" he asked.

"Well, about how Pete and I are going to tell my parents that he's alive and well and neither of us thought to tell them."

"You couldn't tell them, honey," Joel reminded. "You would have put them in danger if you had."

"I know that, but this whole thing just plain sucks. I know that eventually, they'll find a way to forgive both of us, but it will take some time."

"Your parents are going to be so happy that their only son is alive and well, they will forgive you both," Joel assured. "You'll see—it will all work out. Plus, I'll be by your side the whole time, just lean on me if you need to."

"Thanks," she whispered.

"What else are you worried about?" he asked.

"Us," she admitted. "I mean—will there even be an us when this case is over?" she asked.

"Yes," he said without hesitation. "I want there to be an us," he said. "Do you?"

"I do," she admitted. "I was afraid to ask about the whole situation and us living together. I mean, I guess I'll go back to my place once the danger passes."

"I'd rather you don't go back to your place. I mean, you rent, right?" he asked.

"Yes, I have a little apartment in the city," she said.

"Well, I own my place and I'd love for you to move in with me, for real this time. I want you to move in with me because you want to, Trista, and not because there's safety in numbers and we're both in danger."

"I'd like that," she said. She loved his place and found herself daydreaming about living there with him daily. After she moved into his bedroom, she thought that all of her dreams were finally coming true, but then, Trista let self-doubt settle in.

"I would too," he admitted. "So, it's official. You and I are going to shack up once this nightmare with the Gemini Brothers is over, right?" he asked.

Trista giggled, "How romantic," she teased, "you really do have a way with words, Joel."

"Thanks," he said, squeezing her hand into his own. "We're here," he said, nodding to her office building. "You ready for this?"

"No, but we have no choice, right?" she asked. "Are you ready?"

"Yes," Joel said, "I've been waiting to put Dante back in jail since you convinced me to let him out." She understood that. Having a man like Dante free in the world made her sick. He'd hurt so many families, including her own. It was finally time to fix this mess, and then, they'd be able to get on with their lives—and shacking up with Joel as he liked to say.

☠ ☠ ☠

They were given their orders and Henry had everything planned out and everyone in place around the warehouse where Dante and his men were supposedly hidden away with the women that they planned on selling off at auction in the next day or two. This was really happening, and Trista felt every damn butterfly that was fluttering in her tummy.

She usually got this way when she was going into a raid, but this one made her extra antsy.

Joel's team was stationed in the back of the building, and they were going in first. Then, when he gave the all-clear that he was in, her team would move into the front of the warehouse to where Pete promised to meet them and lead her team back to the offices where Dante hung out. If they could pull this off, there would be very little bloodshed, and that was the end goal—especially with so many women being held in cages in the warehouse.

It had been almost five minutes since Joel's team went in, and they were still waiting for the signal for her team to go in. She was feeling antsy and a bit worried about him. She knew that he had a good team surrounding him, including Melody, but she was still worried. When he finally called over the walkie that he was in place, she breathed out the breath she didn't know that she was holding.

"Move in, Trista," Henry said in her ear.

"Let's move," she whispered back to her team. She had just four guys with her, but that was all she'd need with Pete meeting her inside, and Joel's team already in place. As soon as they got through the front entrance, Trista spotted Pete off to the side.

"Hey, Sis," he whispered.

"Don't you hey sis me," she spat. "I'm pissed at you for not calling me, but we'll talk about that later. Where's Dante?" she asked.

"You do know that you're going to have to arrest me too,

right?" he whispered. "I need to keep my cover in case this goes south, and Dante gets out again."

"Well, I will slap handcuffs on you and drag your ass to jail with pleasure," she insisted. "Then, you and I can have a little chat."

"Shit," he mumbled. "I'd like to just go to jail," he teased.

"Too late. You're not a criminal," she said, "although, when I get done with you, you'll wish that you were a criminal."

"Great," he breathed, "follow me," he said. "When we get back there, I'll disappear, and you can arrest me on your way out."

"Fine," she said, "just don't be a douche about being arrested. I don't want to hear you whining."

"Whatever," he grumbled. He led them back to the stairs that led up to the offices. "He's up there," he said nodding to the room with the blinds closed and the faint lights bleeding through. "Be safe, Sis," he said.

"You too," she said, waiting for her brother to disappear into the darkness of the warehouse. Trista motioned to her team to file up the stairs quietly, and when she got to the top, she didn't even give her team a three count, just barging into the office.

Chaos rang out—the gunfire, and shouting was deafening. Trista felt searing pain through her left shoulder, still trudging on to find Dante through the rain of bullets. She quickly looked around the office, noting that Dante was nowhere to be found and that's when it hit her—Pete had double-crossed her. He had fooled them all. He was once again helping Dante to get out of the warehouse, unscathed, and the men that were left behind were expendable. They would go down for human trafficking while Dante would live to fight another day. He'd be able to go on and find another warehouse to fill with women.

"Dante isn't up here," she shouted into her walkie. "Pete's double-crossed us," she yelled. Saying the words out loud made her feel sick, but that had to be what was happening here. He had told her that Dante was up in the office, and he wasn't. Pete didn't stick around when she led her team upstairs to arrest Dante. He was the only variable in the whole case that didn't ever seem to add up. Even when he showed up at Joel's, she wasn't sure if his story seemed plausible. All she could think while he explained what happened to him, was why Dante would agree to keep him alive. That part never really made any sense to her, and now she knew why. Her brother was a double agent. He had double-crossed her and the CIA. He had sent her and her team up those stairs to die tonight while he got away with Dante, and she couldn't let that happen.

"I think Pete went out the West entrance," she shouted into her walkie.

"I'm on it," Joel promised. "I'll find them."

"Don't trust Pete, Joel," she said, "he's working with Dante, I'm sure of it."

"You just get out of there," Joel insisted, "you good?" She looked down at her shoulder, the way that the blood was already soaking her shirt, and she nodded. She was going to have to lie to him, otherwise, Joel would give up on going after Dante and Pete to help her. She'd be fine but letting them go would be a complete waste.

"I'm good," she lied, "just find Dante and Pete."

JOEL

JOEL COULDN'T BELIEVE THAT PETER HAD DOUBLE-CROSSED them all. He had put Trista in danger, and now, he was getting away with Dante. His first instinct was to go to Trista and help her, but there was no way that he'd let Dante get away again, especially now that they knew that Pete was helping him. Joel knew that his girl was tough—he just hoped like hell that she'd be able to handle the shit show that her brother had sent her into.

"You had no idea that Trista's brother was a double agent?" Melody asked.

"None," Joel admitted. "Trista believed her brother too, although, I'm guessing that had more to do with wanting to believe him. She wanted him to be alive and okay so that she could bring him back to her parents, but now, that might not happen."

"You know what we'll have to do if he gives us any fight, right?" Melody asked.

"I do, and that's why I'm glad that we're going after him and not Trista," he admitted. "I just hope that she's okay." The gunfire had stopped ringing out from the upstairs room and there was still no sign of Trista or her team, and that had him worried.

"I'm sure she is," Melody whispered. "From what I know about Trista, she seems very capable of landing on her feet in any circumstance." Melody was right, but he still worried that Trista was keeping something from him when she told him to go after her brother.

They turned the corner and Joel stopped dead when he found Peter standing in the middle of the hallway, holding a gun that was pointed right at him and Melody. "End of the line, guys," he said.

"You don't have to do this Pete," Joel insisted. "Just let us take in Dante and I'm sure that the CIA will strike a deal with you for your cooperation."

"We both know that's not true," Peter insisted. "As soon as I turn over Dante, you'll put me in a cell with him and toss away the key. I have my orders. We need to get the women and Dante out, at any cost."

"Even your sister's life?" Melody spat. "You sent her into that office up there knowing that she'd be facing a firing squad. How could you do that to your own sister?"

"I'm not in charge of my sister or the decisions that she

makes," Peter defended. "She chose to go into that office. I didn't send her anywhere."

"You set her up, and now, we don't know if she's dead or alive," Joel shouted.

Peter shrugged and Joel wanted to tear the asshole apart for what he had just done to Trista. "If she's dead, you are too, Pete," Joel said.

"I don't really do empty threats," Peter said. "I mean, I am the one holding the gun and it's pointed right at you, man," he said.

Joel couldn't help his laugh when he saw Trista round the corner with two of her men. "And Trista is holding a gun and it's pointed right at you," he said nodding at her.

"Good try, asshole," Peter said. "But I'm not letting my guard down and turning around so that you can get the drop on me."

"Suit yourself," Joel said. Trista stood directly behind her brother and when she poked her gun into his back, Pete's gasp filled the small corridor.

"You okay, honey?" Joel asked. He saw the blood that had soaked her shirt and could tell that she had probably been hit in the shoulder.

"I will be as soon as I take care of this trash," Trista spat.

"I'm your brother, Trista," Peter insisted.

"My brother died months ago. My parents and I buried him, and they'll never know that you lied to them. They will never experience the pain and disappointment that their son turned into a traitor. As far as I'm concerned, Pete, you've been dead this whole time." Hearing Trista say those words to her brother broke Joel's heart for her. She was so cold and calculated, but he knew that she was dying on the inside. He'd have to help her deal with all of that later. Right now, he needed to bring down Dante and get Trista some medical attention for her shoulder.

As if she could read his mind, Trista looked around her brother to Joel and nodded. "You and Melody go after Dante. Don't let him go," Trista ordered.

"Be careful, honey," Joel said.

"I always am," she promised. "Cuff him and let's get him into the car. I'm not giving my snake of a brother another chance to get away. He's going to spend the rest of his miserable life in prison."

He knew better than to get in Trista's way. He also knew that she was capable of handling her brother. "Ready?" he asked Melody.

"Yep," she said, following him down the hallway. He was pretty sure that the door at the end of the corridor would lead into the warehouse, and to all of the women that the Gemini Brothers were holding.

He pushed his way through the door, Melody hot on his heels, and found the large room filled with women in cages. Most were crying or calling for help as guards let them out to the trucks that they had waiting for them.

They were going to move the evidence and Joel knew that if they did that, the CIA's case against the Gemini Brothers would be nonexistent. It's why they could only pin Dante down when he was arrested the first time, and they couldn't take the chance that the Gemini Brothers would just put another head in place to lead their family business. Dante might be the acting head, but the Gemini family was large and had many willing men who'd gladly take his place.

"I'll call in back-up," Melody said. "You go after Dante."

"Are you sure?" he asked. He knew that Melody enjoyed the thrill of the chase as much as he did.

"I am," she said, "if we let them move those women, we will have gone through all of this for nothing. We've come too far to let that happen, Joel." Melody was right, although, he'd never tell her that. He'd never hear the end of her "I told you so's" if he did.

"Be careful," he ordered. "Axel will kick my ass if you get shot."

"I'll do my best not to get shot," she said. "You be careful too." He headed over to the dark corner of the building, needing a quiet place to scope out the warehouse for Dante. He spotted the guy almost immediately and was surprised that he didn't have many of his guards around to protect him. He literally let his guard down and Joel knew that he had found his opening, and he wasn't going to waste it.

He hurried along the permitter of the warehouse. Dante seemed distracted watching the women being loaded into the trucks. "Bring in the other truck," he shouted to one of his guys.

"Good plan," Joel said, "looks like you're going to need it." Dante turned around and looked Joel over, his smile was mean. He had his gun pointed at Dante and wasn't sure what the guy had to smile about, but Joel liked to have a bit of fun —he'd play along.

"What's funny?" Joel asked.

"You just don't give up, man. You fucked up the first time arresting me, so now, you're back to try again. You do know that my attorney will have me out again in no time. You've already admitted to failing to follow procedure the first time you brought me in, what makes you think that this time will stick?" he asked.

"Because I'm here to assist," Trista stepped out from the side of the building and Joel was sure that his girl has superpowers.

"What the hell, honey?" he asked. "How did you get here so fast?"

"Well, I took care of the trash, and now that Pete's out of the way, I thought that I'd come on over here and give you a hand. Plus, I wouldn't miss the chance to set the record straight with this asshole."

"Go for it," Joel said. This was going to be fun to watch.

"You're under arrest, Dante Gemini, for human traffick-ing, the murder of two CIA agents," her voice cracked a bit when she said that part, and Joel knew that Trista had left some members of her team up in the office where she had been shot. He listened to her as she read the rest of the charges against Dante Gemini, along with his rights and when she finally finished, the rest of the team was there. Melody had come through and called in backup. She got to them in time to watch him and Trista cuff, Dante. The rest of the team swarmed the building, taking down the guards with very little resistance.

"It's over," he said to Trista.

"It's far from over," she said. "We have a long night of paperwork and questioning ahead of us, Joel."

"No," he said, "you have a trip to the ER to have that shoulder looked at. And then, we're going to get some rest, so that tomorrow, you can hit the ground running—as long as you're medically cleared to do so."

"Joel," she breathed.

"No arguments, Trista," he said. "I love you and I'm not going to stand back and let you bleed out while you do your job."

"Wait—you love me?" she asked.

"I do. I have for a while now, but I didn't want to scare you off," he admitted.

"Why now?" she asked. "What's changed?"

"I heard those gunshots when you went into Dante's office, and God, I thought for sure that I lost you. Hearing that scared the shit out of me. When I heard you tell me that you were okay, I knew that you were lying. I knew that you had to be hit, and that thought terrified me. I knew that I couldn't live without you at that moment. I don't want to be without you, ever. I love you, Trista, and if that scares you— well, too bad."

She smiled up at him, holding her shoulder with her good hand. "It does terrify me, if I'm being honest, Joel. The problem is, I love you too, and I want to spend the rest of my life with you too."

"You do?" he asked. She nodded and he wrapped his arms around her. He felt as though he was holding his whole future in his arms.

"I do," she said.

"Good," he said, "then you'll be willing to say those same words to me when you marry me, honey?" he asked.

"I will," she promised. "I'd love to marry you, Joel."

"Um guys," Melody said, "can we cut the mushy shit short? The ambulance is here and is ready to take Trista to the hospital. I'm assuming that you'll be riding with her, boss?"

"I will be," he agreed. "I'm not leaving her side—ever." He meant it too. Joel had finally found the woman he wanted forever with, and he'd never let her go now that she had agreed to be his.

TRISTA

It had been over two weeks since they brought down the Gemini Brothers and Trista had a quick meeting scheduled with her boss before she was supposed to meet Joel at the courthouse. She told him that she just wanted a simple ceremony—just the two of them, and he complied. She agreed to let her parents throw them a small party for family and friends after they got back from their honeymoon next month. As of tomorrow, they were going to be spending two weeks on a tropical island and that sounded like pure heaven to her.

She walked into Henry's office, and he told her to shut the door. "What's up, boss?" she asked.

"You know that I hate when you call me that, right?" he asked.

"I do, but I just can't seem to help myself," she teased.

"I thought that you should know that I offered Joel a job," he said.

"You offered my soon-to-be husband a job and didn't say anything to me first?" she asked.

"I did, but he turned it down," Henry said.

"What—why would he turn down the chance to work for the CIA?" she asked. There was a knock at the door and Henry called for whomever it was to come in. Joel walked in and she stood from her seat.

"What's going on here?" she asked. Her arm was still in a sling and Joel carefully pulled her good side against his body, wrapping an arm around her waist.

"I thought that I'd come down and pick you up for our little date," he said. They hadn't told anyone except the people closest to them about getting married at the courthouse.

"He knows," she drawled. "I had to tell him since I'm taking the next two weeks off for our honeymoon."

"Congratulations, by the way," Henry said.

"Thanks," Joel breathed. He looked between the two of them, "Did I interrupt something?" he asked.

"Well, you could say that," Trista said, "Henry just told me that he offered you a job here and that you turned it down."

"He did, and I did," Joel admitted.

"Why did you turn it down? I mean, isn't it the next step in your career?" Trista asked.

"Yes, and no," he said. "I've worked so hard to work my way up in the ranks at the precinct. I don't want to leave my position and become the low man on the totem pole over here. While I appreciate the offer, I'm happy where I am. I told you when we met that I love my job, and that hasn't changed. Although my department would be happy to work with yours on future cases if you find it necessary."

"I'll take that into consideration," Henry agreed. "Now, don't you two have a ceremony to get to?"

They had an appointment at the courthouse at two. She checked her watch and nodded. "Yes, and we're going to be late."

"We're only just across the street," Joel said. "I'm sure that we'll make it in time."

"You two have a great honeymoon, and I'll see you when you get back, Trista," Henry said.

"Thanks, boss," she teased. "I should be all healed up by then too." Having her arm in a sling landed her on desk duty, and she was itching to get back out on the street. But first, she planned on marrying the man of her dreams.

"You ready to become my wife?" he asked, reaching for her hand.

Trista took it and smiled up at her soon-to-be husband. "I am," she breathed. "Are you ready to become my husband?" she asked.

"I am," he said, "I've been counting down the minutes, and I can't wait to make you mine, Trista," Joel said.

She giggled, "I hate to tell you this, Joel, but I've been yours since I pulled my gun on you at Savage Hell." She meant it too. She had wanted him from the very beginning and Trista was sure that wouldn't change—ever. Falling for him was an unexpected bonus and becoming his wife was a dream she thought might never come true, but it was. She had finally found her forever, she found her truth, and Trista never planned to let that go again.

The End

I hope you enjoyed Joel and Trista's story. Now, buckle up for your inside sneak peek at Thorne's Rose (Savage Hell Book 8).

ROSE

ROSE SAVAGE WALKED INTO HER COUSIN'S BAR KNOWING THAT she shouldn't have been there but daring to break all of her father's rules. Her dad and Savage's father had a falling out years ago before Savage's father passed. Her dad had forbidden her to step even one toe into Savage Hell, but really, she had no choice. If she wanted to keep her little girl safe, she was going to have to face down the man her father swore was the devil himself.

"Can I help you?" a handsome man behind the bar asked.

"Um, I'm trying to find Savage," she said. "I need his help. Is he around?"

"Well, I guess that depends on who you are," the man challenged. Rose put her hands on her hips and flashed him her best smile. "That's not going to work, honey," he insisted. "I appreciate the pretty smile and all, but no one gets in to see Savage without my approval. So, what's your name, honey?" he asked.

"Rose," she breathed, giving up on her attempt to act sexy for the guy behind the bar. Apparently, he wasn't buying what she was selling. Hell, she hadn't sold anything since before Sadie was born, and that was going on for two years now.

"Rose what?" the man asked. He was starting to sound a bit annoyed with her and she wondered what that was about.

"Rose Savage," she said. "I'm his cousin."

"I see," the man said. "Stay right here, Rose," he ordered, "and don't talk to any of the guys if you know what's good for you."

"What's that supposed to mean?" she shouted over the music, but the guy pretended not to hear her.

Within minutes, the handsome bartender reappeared holding hands with her cousin. At least, Rose thought that it was Savage. He had aged some and was bigger than she remembered him being ten years ago when she last saw him.

"Rose," he breathed. She nodded and Savage picked her up and spun her around. "This is my husband, Bowie," he said, introducing her to the handsome bartender. "I'll introduce you to our wife, Dallas, when she comes in. What are you doing here?" Savage asked.

Hearing that Savage was married to both a man and a woman didn't surprise her much. She had known that her cousin was bi for years. He shared that with her when she was a kid but told her not to tell anyone else. "I need your help," she breathed.

"Of course," Savage agreed, "it's so good to see you."

"Um, you too," she said. "It's been a long time. I'm sorry that I wasn't able to come sooner to visit."

"No, I get it," he said. "Your father has his rules, but why now? I mean, you're breaking his rules now, right?"

"Yes, but he really can't get mad at me anymore," she admitted. She hated having to tell him this part. It wasn't how anyone should find out. "My father passed away over a year ago," she said.

"I see," Savage breathed, "I'm so sorry, Rose. What from?" he asked.

"Heart attack," she whispered. "It was awful. I had just picked up Sadie from daycare and went home to make Dad dinner."

"Who's Sadie?" Savage asked.

Rose smiled, "She's my two-year-old daughter."

"Congratulations," Savage said. "Wow, you're a mom."

"I am," Rose said, "and that's why I need your help. My ex wants custody of her and he's a bad man. If he gets his hands on Sadie, he'll destroy her spirit, and I can't let that happen. He beat me and I know that if given the chance, he'll do the same to her."

"What are his chances of getting custody of her?" Bowie asked.

"Good," Rose whispered, "he's very wealthy and can pay lawyers and keep me in court for ages. I don't have that kind of money. If Sadie has to live with him, I don't know what I'll do."

"All right," Savage said, "of course, I'll help you. What's this guy do for a living?" he asked.

"That's just it," Rose said. "He's a car salesman and a bad one at that. While we were together, he didn't sell many cars. He'd tell me business was slow, but he always had cash on him—a lot of it. He drives high-end cars and lives in a mini mansion. I'm betting that he has a side hustle and that it's not legal."

"I'll need the name of the car lot he works for," Savage said. "I have a few ideas, but this will take a bit of time. Do you and Sadie have someplace safe to go?" Savage asked.

"No, not really," she said. "Every time I try to find a new place, he shows up. It's almost like my ex is staying one step ahead of me all the time."

"We have a guy who can help," Bowie said. "But you'll have to do as he says. He's kind of a control freak, but he's good at keeping people safe. Will you let him help you?" What choice did she have? If she kept trying to run from her ex on her own, he'd eventually catch up to them and take Sadie from her. Rose couldn't let that happen, not after they had come this far.

"I'll accept his help," she breathed.

"Thank you," Savage said. "How about you go pick up your daughter and come on back to our place for dinner? We can call Thorne and get everything set up. He'll meet you at our house and take you and Sadie someplace safe while Bowie and I investigate your ex."

"I don't know how I'll ever repay you for this," Rose admitted. "I'm so grateful that you will help me."

"I don't need payment, Rose. You and Sadie staying safe is payment enough. Thorne is a good guy and I'd trust him with my life. You'll be in good hands," Savage said.

"Word of warning though," Bowie said, "he's a bit rough around the edges. He's all bark and no bite though. Just keep that in mind when you meet him tonight."

"Will do," she agreed. "I'll pick up Sadie from my friend's place and meet you back here in about an hour. Does that work?" Rose asked.

"Yep, and then we can head back to our house. I'll let Dallas know that we'll have two more for dinner," Savage said.

"I don't want to put you or your wife out," she said.

"Not at all," Bowie soothed. "We have a boatload of kids. Two more mouths to feed won't be a problem." She liked hearing that Savage had a family and kids. She had always thought about her cousin as a loner, but she liked seeing him this way—settled down and happy.

"I'm glad that you found happiness," Rose said to Savage. "I'm sorry that we weren't in each other's lives more."

"Well, we couldn't make our fathers get along. And although I tried, I couldn't make your father like me. We'll make up for lost time now, Rose," Savage assured. "You'll find your happiness too, honey, I promise." Rose nodded and turned to leave.

"I'll hold you to that promise, Savage," she whispered to herself on her way out of the bar. She just hoped that it was a promise that he'd be able to keep.

THORNE

Victor Thorne got the call from Savage that he had a gig for him, and he wanted to tell his club's Prez, no, but he also knew that was something he just couldn't do. He had just worked a double shift and he was dog tired.

Since going undercover to root out the trafficking rings in the area, he was burning the candle at both ends. When he joined the CIA, he had no clue how many hours a week he'd be working, and when they stuck him on undercover work, those hours doubled. He barely had time to sleep anymore and that's what he had planned on doing for the next six hours until he had to show back up to work. He was so close to cracking the trafficking ring that he had been working for, he just needed a few more days and then, he'd have the evidence that he'd need to bring down the whole organization and put every scum bag that worked for it behind bars.

He had been doing undercover work for almost eight years now because his boss said that he had the look for it. He knew that his boss took one look at his full upper body tattoos and decided his fate. He was right, Thorne had the look and that was because he used to live that life. He used to be the criminal that he now played, and that gave him a leg up. He knew how the assholes who ran the trafficking rings thought and being able to get into their sick minds was a big part of what made him a damn good CIA agent.

His orders from Savage were that he was supposed to meet him and Bowie over at their house tonight at about six. He knew that turning down his Prez's invitation to come over would be a huge mistake, so he agreed to be there. Apparently, Savage had a family member in trouble and his skills at hiding people away were needed.

Thorne took a quick shower and got dressed, pulling on a clean pair of jeans and a t-shirt. Hopefully, this thing for Savage wouldn't take too long, and then, he'd be able to catch a few hours of sleep before heading back to work in the morning.

He drove over to Savage's house and parked behind Bowie's pick-up. Savage walked out and met him on the front porch, which was never a good sign. It usually meant that he was going to have to talk to Thorne before they got inside and that usually involved some news that he wasn't going to like.

"Hey Savage," he called.

"Thanks for coming out on such short notice," Savage said. "We have a little bit of a situation."

"What kind of situation?" Thorne asked.

"My cousin, Rose, and her two-year-old daughter, Sadie, need to get away for a bit. Her ex is bad news, and she needs to lay low while Bowie and I look into his extracurricular business activities."

"What kind of business activities are we talking about?" Thorne asked.

"He's supposedly a car salesman, but according to my cousin, he'd made too much money for the number of cars that he's selling. Rose is betting that he's involved in a human trafficking ring, but we need time to figure it out."

"I'm betting that will take a bit of time," Thorne said. "Should I plan on this being a long-term thing?"

"Possibly," Savage admitted, "is that going to be a problem?" Thorne wanted to tell Savage that it was going to be a huge problem, but he wouldn't dare. He'd just have to figure out how to juggle his crazy work schedule and help out Savage's cousin, at the same time.

"Not at all," Thorne lied, "I'd be happy to help."

"Great, because I need a place for her and her daughter tonight. She thinks that someone's following her and if that's the case, I can't let her stay here with my family. I won't put them at risk," Savage said. Thorne didn't blame the guy. He would have felt the same way if he had a family to protect, but he didn't.

"Of course," Thorne agreed. "How about I meet your

cousin and her kid and if they're comfortable with every-thing, I can get them into a safe house tonight?"

"That would be wonderful. I'd owe you one, Thorne," Savage said.

"No big deal," Thorne lied. He was sure that helping out Savage's cousin tonight would only lead to him getting no sleep.

Savage nodded, "Follow me," he said. Thorne did as ordered and followed Savage into the back of the house to the kitchen.

"Hey, Thorne," Bowie said. Dallas kissed his cheek and asked if he wanted some dinner, and he lied and said that he had already eaten. The sooner he could meet Rose and get her and her kid settled, the sooner he could crawl into his bed and get some shut eye.

Savage nodded to the petite woman in the corner holding a toddler. "That's my cousin, Rose, and her daughter, Sadie." He took a step toward Rose, and she backed further into the corner. "Rose this is Thorne. He's a friend and you can trust him." She looked at Savage as though he might have lost his mind and Thorne wanted to laugh. He knew what she saw when she looked at him. He was covered in tattoos and looked more like a criminal than someone who was there to save her.

"Good to meet you, Rose," Thorne said. He smiled and waved to the toddler, "You too, Sadie." The little girl smiled back at him and waved. Well, at least one of the women he was going to have to protect seemed to like him.

"You're going to protect us?" Rose asked.

"I am," Thorne said. "If that's okay with you both. I'm good at what I do, and I will have no problem keeping you both safe."

Savage stepped between them and turned to Rose. "Listen, I know Thorne's a bit rough around the edges," he said.

"Gee, thanks for that," Thorne muttered. Savage shot him back a look and turned back to face his cousin.

"We all are," Savage covered, "but, I'd trust Thorne with my life, and I know that he'll keep you and your daughter safe if you'll let him."

"I trust you, Savage," Rose said, "it's why I came to you in the first place. If you say that Thorne will help us, then I trust you. Sadie and I will go with him." She turned to face Thorne and pasted on her best smile. "Thank you for offering to help us."

"Of course," he agreed.

"You'll stay in touch?" Bowie asked Thorne.

"Yes," Thorne agreed, "as soon as I get them settled, I will check in with Savage. I'll keep you guys in the loop."

"Thanks, man," Savage said. "I don't know how I'll ever repay you for doing this for my family."

"I'm sure I'll come up with something," Thorne joked, slapping Savage on the shoulder. He turned back to Rose, "How soon can you be ready?" he asked.

"We're ready now," Rose said. "I just need to change Sadie and then, we can be ready to go with you." She walked past him, and he caught a whiff of her strawberry-scented shampoo and Thorne made a mental note to stop sniffing the pretty girl. If he was going to keep his promise to Savage, he would need to keep his head in the game—strawberry-scented shampoo or not.

Thorne's Rose (Savage Hell Book 8) coming in April 2023!!

Don't miss the other books in the Savage Hell series! These titles are available NOW!

RoadKill -> https://books2read.com/u/bWPeRM
REPOssession -> https://books2read.com/u/bMXDa5
Dirty Ryder -> https://books2read.com/u/3RnyxR
Hart's Desire -> https://books2read.com/u/bpzJ9k
Axel's Grind -> https://books2read.com/u/3Gw9oK
Razor's Edge -> https://books2read.com/u/m0lepY

Trista's Truth-> https://books2read.com/u/med5Rr
Thorne's Rose->Link coming soon!

What's coming next from K.L. Ramsey? You won't want to miss Picture Perfect (The Bridezilla Series Book 2)!

RAINBOW

RAINBOW MEADOWS HAD SPENT MOST OF HER LIFE TRYING TO come up with creative new names to call herself. Kids would tease her mercilessly and when she turned seven, she swore to her parents that she was going to grow up and change her name. Of course, her mother told her that she and Rainbow's father had taken great care in giving her the name Rainbow. Honestly, she wondered just how true that was. How did they miss that her last name was Meadows? She sounded like a total hippy and not a talented photographer that was making quite a name for herself on the local scene.

Rainbow was in high demand as one of the community's best wedding photographers, and she loved her job. She just worried that no one would ever take her seriously after she told them her name. Eventually, she started going by Rain, shortening her birth name, and she had to admit, it seemed to work for her.

Rain walked into her studio that she rented downtown and dumped her bags onto her desk. When she first started working in the photo industry, she couldn't afford a studio. Hell, she could barely afford her studio apartment, but she found a way. Soon, she found herself living in a two-bedroom apartment, using one of the bedrooms as her makeshift office. That all changed once she started booking two or more weddings a weekend. Sure, it was tricky, but when there was a will, there was a way. At least, that's what her mother always told her.

That saying turned out to be her motto in high school when she figured out that she didn't want to go to college. She had to explain to her parents that she wanted to take some photography classes and they convinced her to at least do so at the community college. She ended up with enough credits to get her AA degree and that was enough for her, even if it never seemed to be for either of her parents.

Rainbow's father argued that she had chosen a career that would never pay the rent, and at the time, he was right. But then, she started making money and moved to her two-bedroom apartment, making him eat his words. Maybe that was what she needed—a push to do better, be better, but she wondered if she'd ever be enough. They made her feel like a disappointment at every turn and that plain sucked, even if it pushed her to the next level.

She finally saved enough to have a separate workspace and decided that a studio downtown was the best place to continue to grow her budding business. She loved the street that her office was on—it was always so lively. Her apartment was on a quiet street on the West side of town, but her office was located in the heart of the city where all of the action took place. She loved having the best of both worlds and Rain was sure that she had life all figured out. Well, that was until she got the invite to be the photographer for a wedding in France.

Her favorite wedding planner, Poppy, called her and asked if she'd be willing to photograph a wedding for a client that she had who wanted a destination wedding. Rain had done a few destination weddings—most of them being held on a beach at some tropical location. But she never dreamed that she'd get to shoot a wedding in France. If she allowed herself to dream of the perfect location for a wedding, she'd choose France, but she just never thought that she'd land a gig like that.

Apparently, the bride and groom had an unlimited budget and wanted to bring over a photographer. They said that it would be easier to work with Rain after the actual wedding day was over and they had to discuss edits. They used local talent for flowers, food, spirits, and even the cake. But they wanted an American-based photographer, and for that, Rain was grateful.

The only catch was that the wedding was in just over a

month and she'd have to cancel two other gigs to be in France for the whole weekend. She'd never canceled on any of her clients, but her brain was chanting, "France, France, France," over and over in her head, and what else could she do? She called to cancel her two clients and let Poppy know that she'd be in France with bells on—and well, her camera too, to take pictures of the happy couple's big day. Poppy seemed thrilled, and she was getting a free trip out of the deal—win, win in Rain's book.

She decided to share her exciting news with her parents, wanting to rub it in a bit that she had landed an international photography job, even if her clients were American. Her parents didn't need to know that part though. Rain would keep that information to herself as she shared about her trip to France.

She pulled her cell phone from her pocket and dialed her mother. Out of the two of them, her mom would answer while her dad would let the call go to voicemail every time. He hated answering his cell phone, which caused many fights between her parents.

"Hi, Rainbow," her mother answered. "I knew that it was you because of the caller ID."

"I know, Mom," she said. Caller ID had been around since before Rainbow was even born, yet her mother liked to point out that she knew exactly who was calling her because of the name that popped up on her phone.

"Why are you calling?" her mother asked. "It's not

Wednesday." She usually called her parents on Wednesday, telling them that she was just too busy to call them over the weekend when she was working weddings. Honestly, she was just happy not to get roped into Sunday family dinners because of her job, even if her parents liked to make her feel guilty about that.

"I'm calling to let you know that I have exciting news," Rain said.

"Hold on," her mother said. "Let me get your father so that you can tell us both." She heard her mother rustling around on the other end of the call and sighed. She'd roll her eyes, but Rain knew that it would be a waste of good drama since no one would be able to see her do it.

"Okay, we're both here," her mother said. "Say hello to Rainbow, Frank," her mother ordered.

"Hi, Bow," her father said, calling her the nickname that he'd given her. He started calling her that when she protested having the name Rainbow. Her father was trying to find a compromise, but the name Bow just didn't work for her. It was almost comical that neither of her parents would agree to call her Rain.

"Hi, Dad," Rain said.

"So, what's your exciting news?" her mother asked.

"I've been hired to photograph a wedding in France," she said.

"France," her father repeated. "That's pretty far away, kiddo," he insisted.

"I know, but how exciting is that?" Rain asked. "I mean, I've never left the country before and now, I get to go to France."

"Do you have your passport?" her mother asked.

"Well, not yet," Rain admitted. "But I've done a bit of research, and I can pay to expedite it to make sure that I have it in time. I have a little more than a month before I have to travel, so there's still time."

"Still, sounds like you're cutting it a bit close," her father insisted. This whole conversation wasn't going the way that she had planned. She at least hoped that her parents would be happy for her, if not excited about her trip. But that was just too much to ask from either of them, apparently.

"I'm sure that it will be fine," Rain countered. "Listen, I need to run. I have a client meeting that I can't be late for." That was a total lie, but she was finished with listening to her parent's negativity. She was going to be happy for herself, even if they couldn't seem to be.

She ended the call and sunk into her chair. "Well, that went great," she grumbled. It was her fault, really. She should have savored her good news and kept it to herself instead of sharing it with her negative parents. Lesson learned—at least, that's what she'd tell herself until the next time that she called her parents to share some good news.

Life seemed to slow down to a snail's pace—just like it had every time Rain was waiting for something exciting to happen. But the big day finally rolled around and when she packed her suitcase and her gear to head to France, she felt as giddy as a kid on Christmas Eve. She had waited for this day for a little over a month now and stepping on the plane was the most exciting moment of her life. She just had no idea how big of a step it was going to be for her or how much her life was going to change—but boy was it going to.

DUSTIN

DUSTIN SHIELDS WASN'T LOOKING FORWARD TO HIS OLDEST brother's wedding. The only good thing about the "Big day" as his overzealous mother liked to call his brother's wedding day, was the fact that they were getting hitched in France. Maybe a change of scenery would be just what he needed to finally get over being dumped by Daisy. She was supposed to be "The one" according to his mother, but she turned out to like screwing around on him, more than she liked the idea of spending forever as his wife. He asked and having her turn him down hurt like hell until the other men in her life started coming out of the woodwork. That was when Dustin realized that he had dodged a bullet by not marrying Daisy. She would never be faithful to him and when she admitted that to him, he ran as far as he possibly could from her—

moving from California back home to his parent's home in New York.

It took him months not to miss Daisy every day, and even more, time to not think about her every single day. It was a work in progress and being back home helped, except for when his mother reminded him that he wasn't getting any younger and was the last of her five sons to not settle down. Until now, his oldest brother, Darrin held that title, but once he got married this weekend, Dustin would be the only one of them left—the bachelor of the family. Sure, he'd be the social pariah of the family gatherings and holidays, but he really didn't give a fuck. He wouldn't push himself to find a wife if he wasn't ready to take that step—not again. He needed time to figure out what he wanted in life, and what he wanted from a relationship, and then, he'd start looking again.

Dustin got on with the rest of his life, not wanting to live in his parent's home forever, he found a job at one of the top accounting firms in town and even bought a house about ten minutes from his mom and dad's place. It was far enough to give himself privacy but close enough to be there for the both of them if they should need him.

He was on his way home from work when his cell phone rang. Dustin pulled into his driveway and pulled the phone from his pocket, seeing his brother's face on the screen.

"Hey Darrin," he said.

"You about ready to party in France?" his brother asked.

"I just got home from work, so no," Dustin admitted.

"Yeah, crunching numbers sounds like a ton of fun, but we're talking France, man," Darrin reminded. His brothers like to give him a ton of shit about becoming an accountant. He loved his job though and crunching numbers, as his brother liked to call it, was something that he absolutely loved. In fact, he couldn't imagine doing anything else.

"Are you sure that it's okay for me to stay at Danielle's parent's home? I'd be happy getting a hotel room like the rest of the guests," Dustin said. The bride-to-be was from France and the main reason why the wedding ceremony and reception were being held there. Her family owned a beautiful chateau where the wedding was being held and everyone from the bridal party was invited to stay at the chateau, along with his parents. Dustin was honestly not looking forward to staying with his entire family at the chateau. The last time that the five brothers and parents went on vacation together, they rented a huge beach house and everyone—spouses, kids, even dogs, all stayed under the same roof. It was a long damn week and one that he couldn't wait to end. After that trip, Dustin promised himself that he wasn't going to go on another family trip where they all stayed under one roof—yet here he was.

"Don't worry," Darrin said. "You'll have your own personal space. I've made sure to keep you as far away from all of our nieces and nephews this time."

"Thanks for that," Dustin said. "I still have scars from my

last run-in with those little devils." All the kids thought that their beach vacation was the perfect opportunity to beat the crap out of Uncle Dustin. They were vicious too, and he had no desire to repeat their week of torture while they were all staying in France.

"So, we'll see you at the airport in the morning?" his brother asked.

"Yeah, I'll be there," he said.

"Great, see you in the morning. Don't be late—remember, it's an international flight and you need to be there a couple of hours before we're due to board." He already knew all of that, but his oldest brother was the bossy one of the bunch, and he knew that it was best just to let him fulfill his role in the family.

"Got it," Dustin assured. "I'll see you in the morning, Darrin." He ended the call and walked into his house, needing to figure out dinner and hopefully have a few beers while he packed. It was going to be a long week, and he was already looking forward to the flight home.

He spent most of his first days in France having his future sister-in-law bark orders at him, telling him what he needed to do. Dustin knew that Danielle just wanted her wedding day to be perfect, but he was jet-lagged and crabby, and a nap sounded like just what he needed. He decided to try to sneak off to his room on the second floor of the chateau when Darrin found him.

"Where are you going?" he asked.

"Um, bathroom," he lied.

"You've always been a bad liar, Dustin," his brother accused. "We have to go to town and try on our tuxedos. We have the final fitting so that we can pick them up in two days. Plus, I need to pick up our wedding planner, Poppy, and the wedding photographer at the airport."

"Can't you do all of that stuff on your own? I'm exhausted," Dustin said.

"No, I can't. I'm just as tired as you are, so stop your whining," he said.

"Right, but you're living in a love bubble and I'm not. I'm sure that your bride-to-be is worth losing sleep over for you, but that's not the case for me."

"Well, thank God for that," Darrin said. "Otherwise, I'd have to kick your ass. Let's go get the tuxedos. I can't be late picking up Poppy or Danielle will kill me." Dustin mumbled something under his breath about wedded bliss and Darrin shot him a look.

By the time they got to the airport, they were twenty minutes late and his poor brother couldn't seem to apologize enough to the wedding planner and her sexy photographer. Honestly, when Darrin said the words, "Wedding photographer," he instantly conjured the picture of an old, fat, balding guy. He wasn't sure why that was—probably because his three other brothers' wedding photographers seemed to fit that description.

He and his brother loaded their gear and bags into the car and Dustin slipped into the back of the car with the photographer. Poppy sat shotgun with Darrin so that he'd be able to catch her up with what was happening around the chateau.

Dustin held out his hand to the pretty photographer, "I'm Dustin. I'm the groom's brother," he said.

She placed her hand into his and shook it. "I'm Rain," she said.

"That's an unusual name," he said. She quickly pulled her hand from his and buckled her seatbelt.

"You have no idea," she breathed.

"What?" he asked, not sure that he had heard what she said.

"My name is really Rainbow Meadows, but I shortened it to Rain."

"Wow," he breathed, "that is different but in a good way."

"If you say so. But having to grow up with that name has been a challenge, to say the least." He knew just how mean kids could be and having to deal with a different name would make her stand out.

"Yeah, kids can be assholes," he said. "I mean, wait until you meet my nieces and nephews."

She giggled, "You don't like kids?" she asked.

"It's not that I don't like kids, I just don't like the ones who are related to me, wanting to make my life miserable."

"They like to gang up on Dustin. He's the youngest

brother in our family and well, the kids think that he's one of them," Darrin said.

"But I'm a grown man," Dustin insisted. "And I'm sick of sitting at the kid's table at family dinners."

Rain laughed again, "You sit at the kid's table for family dinner?" she asked. "How old are you?"

"I'm twenty-six years old, but I'm also the youngest of five brothers and that garners me a seat at the kid's table," Dustin grumbled. "It's time for me to move to the adult table, but I think my mother's punishing me for being a bachelor."

"So, no kids or wife then?" Rain asked.

"Nope," Dustin said. "How about you?" he asked. "Do you have a family waiting for you back at home?"

"Not unless you count two parents who are very disappointed about my life choices," she said.

"I don't think that's true," Dustin insisted. "I mean, look at you, what could they possibly be disappointed about?"

"Oh, you'd be surprised," she said. "I guess they never saw me becoming a photographer, but I love it, so there's that."

"Well, loving what you do is important. My brothers love to give me shit about being an accountant, but I love my job too, so it doesn't matter to me what they say."

"Right," she agreed. "Plus, I get to photograph this wedding in France, so that should have really shut my parents up, but it didn't. I've already decided to enjoy myself while I'm here. I mean, when will I get the chance to come to France again?"

"So, this trip isn't all about work for you then?" he asked, suddenly coming up with a damn good plan to give him a chance with her.

"Nope," she said. "I plan on having a whole lot of fun while I'm here too."

"Great," he said, "then how about being my date for the wedding?"

She giggled, "Um, I have to take photographs, remember? It's kind of what I'm getting paid to do here."

"Right, but you just said that you were going to have some fun while you were working. I just thought you'd find a way to do both," he admitted.

"Well, my motto is, 'When there's a will, there's a way,' so I'd love to be your date as long as you're okay with me working while I'm on our date."

"That works for me," he agreed. "And I'm fine with you having to work on our date as long as you save me a dance or two."

"Deal," she agreed, holding her hand out to him. He took hers into his own and shook it. He wasn't sure how he was going to get through his brother's wedding without a date and now, he had an evening to look forward to with the sexiest wedding photographer that he'd ever met. Things were finally looking up for Dustin and he had a feeling that he was going to like France.

Picture Perfect Universal Link-> https://books2read. com/u/mY6l2P

You, my lucky reader, are in for a treat (No tricks here!)! K.L. is also sharing another book that will be released in September 2022! Do you love the Royal Bastards? How about an RBMC involving (my favorite holiday) Halloween? Here's a sneak peek at Possessing Demon (Royal Bastards MC: Huntsville, AL Chapter Book 8)!

DEMON

DEMON WALKED INTO SAVAGE HELL AND LOOKED AROUND. IF he didn't find Savage, he was sure that all hell was going to break loose and that was the last thing that he needed. It had already been a shittastic week, and now this.

"You look lost," Bowie said from behind the bar. If anyone would know where Savage was, it would be his husband, Bowie. "You need a beer?" he asked.

"Beer's not going to cut it," Demon admitted. "You have anything stronger?"

"Well, you know that Savage keeps the good stuff back in his office. Should I go back and get it?" Bowie asked.

"Is he back there?" Demon asked, nodding to the back of the bar.

"He is, but I have to warn you, he's not in a good mood. He's probably already hitting up the good stuff, and you know how misery loves company, right?" He had to admit, he was already pretty damn miserable himself.

"I'm not sure which one of us will be misery and which will be company, but I'll take my chances," Demon said.

"It's your funeral, man," Bowie teased. He gave Demon a mock salute and shook his head at him. Demon had no other choice in the matter. He needed to talk to Savage about the shitstorm that was about to hit the Royal Bastards. His Prez had a right to know about it before it happens.

Demon knocked on the closed office door, not sure how he was going to even get the words out. Every time he thought about it, he wanted to punch something, and he had a feeling that Savage was going to feel the same way about it.

"I told you that I need some time, Bowie," Savage growled. "Leave me the fuck alone and I'll come to you when I'm ready to talk." Well, shit, Bowie wasn't completely truthful with him when he said that Savage was in a bad mood. He was in a fucking awful mood, and it had to do with a domestic issue that he was walking right into the middle of.

"It's not Bowie, man," he shouted back, "it's Demon and we need to talk." Savage slurred together a string of curses on the other side of the door and Demon wasn't sure if he wanted to laugh or haul ass out of there for his own self-preservation. But this news couldn't wait—he knew it and walking into that office was the only way to make sure that nothing else happened to any of their members or their women.

Savage pulled open his office door, his expression murderous, and he waved Demon in. "This better be good," he warned.

"It is," Demon promised. "We have trouble and I need to know how you want me to handle it."

"Shit, Demon," Savage grumbled. "I already have enough damn trouble, what now?"

"You might want to take another drink of that and have a seat, boss," Demon said, nodding to the open bottle of whiskey on his desk.

Savage grabbed down two shot glasses and poured them each a drink. "You look like you could use this too," he said, handing it over to him.

"Thanks, man," Demon said. "I could use more than just this, but it's a start."

"Want to tell me what's going on?" Savage asked. He didn't. Hell, Demon didn't even want to think about what had happened, but there would be no denying it once the local press got ahold of it.

"I got a call from Joel," he said. "You know he's a cop, right?" he asked. It was a stupid question. Savage knew everything that there was to know about each of their patched members. He was the club's Prez, and it was his job to be in everyone's business.

Savage shrugged, "Sure," he said, "what about him?"

"Well, he gave me a head's up that one of the guys was found dead on the side of route 72," Demon said.

"Shit—who was it?" Savage asked. "And why wasn't I called in first?"

"Because Joel knows what I do for the club. He knew that I'd need to be called in to take a look at the scene, under the radar, before he called it in. It was Spider," he breathed. He could still see the guy laying in the ditch every damn time that he closed his fucking eyes. It was something that he'd never be able to forget, no matter how much he drank trying to do just that.

"Fuck," Savage shouted. "He just got out of prison. What the hell happened? Was it a bike accident?"

"No," Demon said. "It wasn't an accident. It was murder and his bike was nowhere to be found. Whoever killed him did it someplace else and then dumped his body in the ditch on the side of the road."

"Does Joel know who did it?" Savage asked.

"Not officially, but this was tossed on top of the body." He handed Savage a patch that said "Ghost" across it. He knew that they were involved, he just had no idea what they wanted and what Spider had to do with any of it.

"The fucking Ghosts did this?" Savage asked.

"There's more," Demon said.

"Great," Savage grumbled. "Let's have it."

"There are rumblings around town that the Ghosts are coming for Savage Hell. My source said that they've pledged to bring down the Royal Bastards from the top down, starting with our city. Spider was just the first, and I aim to keep him as the last member that they fucking touch."

"Agreed," Savage growled. "How do we fucking do that?" he asked. Another knock sounded at the door and Savage let out a few more curses, walking over to it and pulling it open. Joel was standing on the other side, in the hallway, and a woman with long, brown hair stood next to him. Her lip was busted, and she looked scared out of her damn mind.

"What's going on, Joel?" Demon asked before Savage got the chance.

"This is my sister, Luna," Joel said. "She's in trouble and I could use some help."

"What the fuck happened," Savage asked.

"The Ghosts happened. They found out that I'm her brother when it was released to the press that I'm the acting detective on Spider's case. They also found out that I'm in the Royal Bastards and well, they decided to question my little sister about it. They roughed her up pretty good, and I can't keep an eye on her and work this case. I think that was what they were hoping for—to get me off the case."

"You know we've got you, man," Savage offered. "You need to find out who killed Spider and Demon will watch Luna. It's what he does for the club, man. Your sister is a part of us, no matter what, Joel, and we take care of our own."

"Do I have a say in any of this?" Luna mumbled.

"No," the three men said in unison.

"So much for women's lib," she grumbled. She walked past Savage and Demon to plop down on the leather sofa that sat in the corner of the small office. "I'm twenty-three years old, Joel, and I don't need your biker groupie friends babysitting me. I can handle myself."

"Sure, just like you did today. You look in the mirror lately, sis?" Joel asked. "Because your eye is getting blacker and more swollen by the second—same with your lip." She reached up and gently touched her swollen face and Demon almost felt bad for the kid.

"It's all right, kid," he said. "I'll keep an eye on you and will try not to cramp your style too much, deal?" he asked.

Luna barked out her laugh, "You're like what, five years older than I am and you're calling me kid?" she asked.

"Actually, I'm ten years older than you, and yeah, that makes you a kid, Luna," he said.

"Listen, guys," Joel started, "I have to get back down to headquarters. I need to follow up on a few leads and talk to my boss about Spider's case. Can you please just sit on her and keep her from doing anything stupid?" he asked.

"What about my job, Joel?" she asked. "I can't just not show up."

"I'll stop down at the tattoo shop and tell Rico that you won't be in for a while. I'll tell him that you caught mono and are really contagious. That guy fucking hates germs and will agree to give you some time off to save his own ass from getting sick." Luna crossed her arms over her chest and stared her brother down as if that worked for her in the past. It was almost comical to watch her trying to take on her older brother. Demon was pretty sure that she was fighting a losing battle, but he wouldn't be the one to tell her that.

LUNA

"You can't be serious," she spat. "You know that he'll fire me if I don't show up for days on end." She was giving her older brother her best angry scowl and from the amused expressions on the guys' faces, none of them were buying it. She wasn't sure if she even bought it because she was a total liar.

When the guy from the Ghosts showed up at her place, she wasn't sure what to do. At first, she thought that he was one of the guys from her brother's club. He looked the part, but then, when he dragged her out of her apartment by the hair, threatening to kill her, she realized that she had misjudged him. Most of the guys that she had met from Savage Hell seemed pretty chill and the guy who was pounding on her face didn't give her very chill vibes.

"I'm sorry, Luna," Joel said. "I know that none of this is

fair to you. They came for you because of who I am and my involvement in this case and this club. But I can't do my job and worry about you."

"What about Trista?" Savage asked. "If they found your sister, they'll find your woman too."

"She's safe," he said. "She's visiting her parents and helping her mother to get back on her feet after her surgery. I'll call her to fill her in, but you know that my girl is hardcore. She'll be able to watch her six."

"Oh, sure," Luna sassed, "just because Trista's a CIA agent, she gets to do whatever she wants and keep her freedom. But since I work for a tattoo parlor, I have to be babysat by grandpa over there," she said, nodding to Demon.

He barked out his laugh and she wasn't sure why he thought that the insult was so damned funny. "It was an insult, asshole," she spat.

"Yeah, I got that," the old guy said. "But you can call me Demon. I'm still a bit too young to answer to grandpa."

"Jesus, Luna," Joel grumbled, "try to behave. I'll check in on you later. Don't give him too much trouble."

"I'm sure that if I do, he'll put me in a time-out or take away the television," she shouted back at her brother.

"Sorry, man," he said to Demon, "she's usually not this much of a handful. If you need me, you know how to get me. Don't let her out of your sight—she's tricky sometimes."

"Not a chance," Demon said. "I'll duct tape her ass to a chair if I need to, don't you worry, man," he assured. "She's not going anywhere." Joel crossed the room and gently kissed her cheek. Luna knew that she winced in pain, but she couldn't help it, and if her older brother felt just a little bit bad about causing her pain, then she was fine with it.

"I'll see you soon, Sis," he promised.

"Whatever," she mumbled under her breath. Joel sighed and left the office, leaving her sitting there with her new protector. The big older guy followed her brother out of the office, and she could hear that they were having a muffled conversation outside in the hallway. She strained her ears, trying to listen to what they were saying, but Luna had no luck eavesdropping.

"So, besides being trouble, you're nosey too?" Demon asked.

"What I am and am not is none of your fucking business, Grandpa," she spat. Yeah, she was being a bitch, but she didn't care. Luna didn't ask for any of this shit. She was just going about her day when that asshole from the Ghosts came to beat the shit out of her, and now, she was regretting calling her brother for help after he left. If she would have just kept all of this mess to herself, she wouldn't need a babysitter. And no matter how attractive she thought Grandpa was, she didn't need a fucking protector.

"How about you sit tight and let me work a few things out and then, we'll get out of here," Demon offered.

"Fine," she said, crossing her arms tighter over her chest. He looked her over and laughed, walking out to the hallway to join the conversation that her brother and the old guy were having.

She wished she had her phone, but Joel took that from her, along with her purse and car keys. He was treating her like a child, and she couldn't do a damn thing about it. Instead, she was supposed to sit on the sofa at a dive bar and behave herself. Yeah, that shit wasn't going to fly with her.

Luna listened for the hushed voices, making sure that the three guys were still talking, and then decided to try the window. She stood and tiptoed over to the office's only window, tugging at the locks, but they wouldn't budge.

"Shit," she whispered.

"Oh yeah," Demon said from behind her. "Your brother's right, you're going to give me trouble at every turn, aren't you, honey?"

"I'm not your honey, asshole," she spat. "And I can save you a whole bunch of trouble. All you have to do is just let me go, and problem solved. You won't have any more trouble and I won't have an asshole for a babysitter."

"Well, I have to say, I like being called an asshole a whole lot more than I liked being called Grandpa," he said. "Since you're so eager to get outside, I think it's time that we high-tailed it out of here."

"Who the hell talks like that?" she sassed. "Now, you're just trying to sound old, aren't you?"

"You know, I like a good challenge, Luna," Demon said. "And you know what I like to do to little girls who talk shit?"

She wasn't sure if she wanted to know the answer to his question or not. She shrugged and his smile grew mean. "I warm their asses until they learn to behave. Tell me that you'll need me to do that for you, Luna," he begged. "My hand is just itching to smack that sweet ass of yours to teach you a lesson."

She gasped and reached around to cover her ass with her hands. "You wouldn't dare," she challenged.

"See now, you don't know me, Luna," he said. "But if you did, you'd know that I would dare. Try me, honey," he said. "I dare you." He might not back down from a challenge, but she never backed down from a fucking dare.

"Dare accepted, Grandpa," she sassed. Demon huffed out his breath and grabbed her arm.

"You had to push, didn't you, honey?" he asked. She knew that he wasn't looking for a response to his question.

"What are you going to do?" Luna breathed.

"You'll see soon enough, honey," he promised. She wasn't sure if she was scared out of her mind or turned on. Probably a bit of both and from the way Demon was looking at her, he knew it too.

ABOUT K.L. RAMSEY & BE KELLY

Romance Rebel fighting for
Happily Ever After!

K. L. Ramsey currently resides in West Virginia (Go Mountaineers!). In her spare time, she likes to read romance novels, go to WVU football games and attend book club (aka-drink wine) with girlfriends. K. L. enjoys writing Contemporary Romance, Erotic Romance, and Sexy Ménage! She loves to write strong, capable women and bossy, hot as hell alphas, who fall ass over tea kettle for them. And of course, her stories always have a happy ending. But wait—there's more!

Somewhere along the writing path, K.L. developed a love of ALL things paranormal (but has a special affinity for shifters <YUM!!>)!! She decided to take a chance and create another persona- BE Kelly- to bring you all of her yummy shifters, seers, and everything paranormal (plus a hefty dash of MC!).

K. L. RAMSEY'S SOCIAL MEDIA

Ramsey's Rebels - K.L. Ramsey's Readers Group
https://www.facebook.com/groups/ramseysrebels

KL Ramsey & BE Kelly's ARC Team
https://www.facebook.com/
groups/klramseyandbekellyarcteam

KL Ramsey and BE Kelly's Newsletter
https://mailchi.mp/4e73ed1b04b9/authorklramsey/

KL Ramsey and BE Kelly's Website
https://www.klramsey.com

f facebook.com/kl.ramsey.58

⊙ instagram.com/itsprivate2

BB bookbub.com/profile/k-l-ramsey

𝕏 twitter.com/KLRamsey5

a amazon.com/K.L.-Ramsey/e/B0799P6JGJ

BE KELLY'S SOCIAL MEDIA

BE Kelly's Reader's group
https://www.facebook.com/
groups/kellsangelsreadersgroup/

facebook.com/be.kelly.564

instagram.com/bekellyparanormalromanceauthor

twitter.com/BEKelly9

bookbub.com/profile/be-kelly

amazon.com/BE-Kelly/e/B081LLD38M

WORKS BY K. L. RAMSEY

The Relinquished Series Box Set

Love Times Infinity

Love's Patient Journey

Love's Design

Love's Promise

Harvest Ridge Series Box Set

Worth the Wait

The Christmas Wedding

Line of Fire

Torn Devotion

Fighting for Justice

Last First Kiss Series Box Set

Theirs to Keep

Theirs to Love

Theirs to Have

Theirs to Take

Second Chance Summer Series

True North

The Wrong Mister Right

Ties That Bind Series

Saving Valentine

Blurred Lines

Dirty Little Secrets

Ties That Bind Box Set

Taken Series

Double Bossed

Double Crossed

Double The Mistletoe

Double Down

Owned

His Secret Submissive

His Reluctant Submissive

His Cougar Submissive

His Nerdy Submissive

His Stubborn Submissive

Alphas in Uniform

Hellfire

Royal Bastards MC

Savage Heat

Whiskey Tango

Can't Fix Cupid

Ratchet's Revenge

Patched for Christmas

Love at First Fight

Dizzy's Desire

Possessing Demon

Mistletoe and Mayhem

Legend

Savage Hell MC Series

Roadkill

REPOssession

Dirty Ryder

Hart's Desire

Axel's Grind

Razor's Edge

Trista's Truth

Thorne's Rose

Lone Star Rangers

Don't Mess With Texas

Sweet Adeline

Dash of Regret

Austin's Starlet

Ranger's Revenge

Heart of Stone

Smokey Bandits MC Series

Aces Wild

Queen of Hearts

Full House

King of Clubs

Joker's Wild

Betting on Blaze

Tirana Brothers (Social Rejects Syndicate

Llir

Altin

Veton

Dirty Desire Series

Torrid

Clean Sweep

No Limits

Mountain Men Mercenary Series

Eagle Eye

Hacker

Widowmaker

Deadly Sins Syndicate (Mafia Series)

Pride

Envy

Greed

Lust

Wrath

Sloth

Gluttony

Forgiven Series

Confession of a Sinner

Confessions of a Saint

Confessions of a Rebel

Chasing Serendipity Series

Kismet

Sealed With a Kiss Series

Kissable

Never Been Kissed

Garo Syndicate Trilogy

Edon

Bekim

Rovena

Billionaire Boys Club

His Naughty Assistant

His Virgin Assistant

His Nerdy Assistant

His Curvy Assistant

His Bossy Assistant

His Rebellious Assistant

Grumpy Mountain Men Series

Grizz

Jed

Axel

A Grumpy Mountain Man for Xmas

The Bridezilla Series

Happily Ever After- Almost

Picture Perfect

Haunted Honeymoon for One

Rope 'Em and Ride 'Em Series

Saddle Up

A Cowboy for Christmas

WORKS BY BE KELLY (K.L.'S ALTER EGO...)

Reckoning MC Seer Series

Reaper

Tank

Raven

Reckoning MC Series Box Set

Perdition MC Shifter Series

Ringer

Rios

Trace

Perdition 3 Book Box Set

Silver Wolf Shifter Series

Daddy Wolf's Little Seer

Daddy Wolf's Little Captive

Daddy Wolf's Little Star

Rogue Enforcers

Juno

Blaze

Elite Enforcers

A Very Rogue Christmas Novella

One Rogue Turn

Graystone Academy Series

Eden's Playground

Violet's Surrender

Holly's Hope (A Christmas Novella)

Renegades Shifter Series

Pandora's Promise

Kinsley's Pact

Leader of the Pack Series

Wren's Pack

Printed in Great Britain
by Amazon

87879292R00098